NOTES FROM THE COUNTRY CLUB

BOOKS BY KIM WOZENCRAFT

Rush

Notes from the Country Club

KIM WOZENCRAFT

NOTES FROM THE COUNTRY CLUB

HOUGHTON MIFFLIN COMPANY

BOSTON   1993   NEW YORK

For information about permission to
reproduce selections from this book, write to
Permissions, Houghton Mifflin Company,
215 Park Avenue South,
New York, New York 10003.

Library of Congress Cataloging-in-Publication Data
Wozencraft, Kim.
Notes from the country club / Kim Wozencraft.
p.   cm.
ISBN 0-395-62892-X
I. Title.
PS3573.O98N6   1993
813'.54 — dc20   93-13007
CIP

Printed in the United States of America

AGM 10 9 8 7 6 5 4 3 2 1

To my mother

Like the church
Like a cop
Like a mother
You want me to be truthful.
　　— Joni Mitchell,
　　　"The Same Situation"

ACKNOWLEDGMENTS

My heartfelt thanks to:

Karen Amos, Debra Cohen, Ivan Fisher, Kristen Hamilton, Elliot Hoffman, Heather Schroder, and Deirdre and Mel Wulf. I especially want to thank Betsy Lerner and Amanda Urban; my husband, Richard Stratton, and our son, Maxwell.

NOTES FROM THE COUNTRY CLUB

1 Nina says the secret to being a lady is to keep your knees slightly bent.

"Even when you walk," she says, "never straighten them completely." She drops next to me on the couch in the dayroom, running one hand through freshly dyed blond hair. "Advice from my mother," she says. "Smartest thing she ever told me."

She is doing five years for paperhanging, Nina, and when she finishes her federal time, she'll have bench warrants waiting for her in nine different states. Two of them have already put holds on her. The authorities will have to fight over who gets her first.

She told me the day I came in that her only offense was partying her way across the United States. "But just as we drove into Reno," she said, "lightning hit the proverbial outhouse." Nina is, or was, a master at passing bad checks, and sees Dr. Hoffman twice a week in forty-minute sessions behind the cloudy glass door of his office.

"Remember," she says now, "you heard it from me. How long did you say your sentence was, anyway?"

I notice that Harold is only pretending to read the newspaper. He sits in the corner of the room, his corner, with his ears pricked in our direction. Harold is a hack; that is what they call guards in this place. He said inmates must call him Mr. Kojak, but none of them do, so I don't either.

"Nina," I say, "I've told you. I'm only here for an evaluation. I'm here to prove my competence. They said six weeks."

"And what, it's been three already? Good luck, girlfriend. Where'd you catch your case?" This as though it were something contagious.

"Right here in Texas."

"Six weeks, eh?" Her laugh is a honey-sweet drawl that starts in Georgia and winds its way to somewhere around Trenton, New Jersey, ending with a choking, coughing ack-ack-ack. I'm not certain why the Feds have her here instead of in the main compound, but I do know that she often has days when she does nothing but eat, smoke and cry.

"So where'd you leave your accent?" she asks. "You don't talk like any Texan I've heard in recent history."

I tell her I spent most of my twenties living at Riverside and Eighty-eighth, which seems to please her.

"Ah, the Apple." She smiles. Then, in a lilting, reasonably good mimic of a southern Black accent: "New York City. Jest like I pictured it. Skyscrapers an' everything."

I remain in place, staring at something on the TV screen while Nina scuffs toward the stairs, pulling a cigarette from the pocket of her fluffy blue chenille bathrobe. Size eight. I have an eye for these things.

"What time is it?" she yawns. "When is my appointment? And where's Herlinda hiding?" She hangs the cigarette between her lips and leans her way through the yellow doors to the stairwell, looking as though she is being led by her unlit smoke.

Only hacks and nurses carry matches, though sometimes one of the Cuban women, usually Herlinda, will have a pack. She has them smuggled in from the main population for her religious ceremonies, furtive occurrences that fall somewhere between voodoo and American Catholicism.

"Not quite one, sweetheart; you see him at three o'clock." Herlinda's voice floats through the stairwell doors, and I hear Nina's reply banging off the yellow-painted cinder block walls.

"Two entire hours," she moans. "Eternity. What am I going to do for two whole, complete, entire, unmitigated motherfucking hours. And why's he wasting time with Three Sheets, anyway? Got a match?"

If it is not quite one, I should go downstairs, back to work, but I don't move. Dr. Hoffman has reserved his one o'clock slot on Tuesdays and Thursdays for Three Sheets, a fortyish matron who's in for bludgeoning her husband. She's doing a life sentence and has been here for as long as anyone can remember, longer even than Glenda, who's been here nearly four years. Nina swore to me early on that Three Sheets had used a GE steam iron. "His head must have looked like road pizza," she said, "but, hey, they bring good things to life."

Three Sheets stays in 301, the room three doors down from mine on the third floor. She spends exactly four hours each day hand-polishing to radiance a nine-square-foot section of the floor outside her room, using tiny wads of toilet tissue to shine each individual linoleum tile. Dr. Hoffman has her doing the Thorazine shuffle, slow-dancing through the minutes. Perhaps that is why we call her Three Sheets.

Nina and I have agreed that, unlike Three Sheets, we are not prone to hallucinations. We have seen for ourselves that the doctor really does wear his wristwatch on his right ankle. Neither of us has yet asked him why, but we have decided that we appreciate his attempt to keep time off our minds. The flourishing grapevine that winds through the halls has it that Dr. H works here because he was arrested in Saint Louis for being too liberal with prescriptions.

I hear Nina coming back up the stairs now, the slow sandpaper sound of her slippers against the safety treads on each step. Her cigarette is finally lit and she glides, bent-kneed, around the dayroom looking for something to use as an ashtray. She settles for a gum wrapper, which she folds into a careful square, foil side up, before sitting down next to me. Chewing gum, like matches, is contraband, which makes it something worth coveting.

She is doing this to try to make Harold angry, but he ignores her, instead taking a cigarette from his own pocket and making a big show of using his plastic lighter. After adjusting the flame to the size of a small blowtorch he touches it to his cigarette and takes a long serious drag before pocketing the lighter and pretending to return to his paper. Nina ignores him.

"You know," she says, "the fucking *federales* got me in the Apple, though no place nearly so cool as Riverside Drive. The Southern District of New York, that was the end for me. While I was staying with this guy who had this really tiny apartment. His view was incredible, though; it looked right out at a big healthy chunk of the city. Did you like it there?"

"Loved it," I say.

"Yeah. Drag. It was weird, though, with this guy. He wasn't exactly in tune with how the cow ate the cabbage, don't you know. Every evening, just at dusk, he would put on Boz Scaggs singing 'Somebody Loan Me a Dime' and get down on his knees and arms on this old blue sort of oriental rug he had, and stare out the window at the Chrysler Building." She flips an ash in the general direction of the gum wrapper. "When I asked him what he was praying for," she says, "he told me it wasn't what you prayed *for* that was important, it was who you prayed *to*. Said any truly good prayer is always two things. Gracious and simple." She raises a blond eyebrow at me, smirks. Then, with a sigh, "I don't know." She says, "All I ever heard him say was 'Thank you, Lee.' "

She stops talking long enough to blow an oval smoke ring and watch it float toward the insulated ceiling as Three Sheets baby-steps her way across the dayroom to the hall. Then she closes her eyes and lets her head rest on the back of the couch.

"Yeah," she says, "he was a real trip."

"What happened to him?"

"Who knows? Not me. I haven't seen him or heard from him since the Feds grabbed my ass."

I tell her I'm late for work.

"Cynthia," Harold says, listening in as usual and momentarily roused from his stupor, "get your butt downstairs."

"Lace those bags," Nina drawls. "Work for the Uncle. I love it."

I pull myself up from the couch, wondering how to part company. "What are you doing for dinner?" I ask. She sighs again and gets up to change the channel. At least I got her to smile. I always feel better when the others smile.

The air in the stairwell is humid and warm. I push my way through the gymnasium smell to the first floor. The windows in the workroom reach almost from floor to ceiling. We have a view of the courtyard.

I work because Dr. Hoffman feels it is essential if he is to evaluate me properly. So, along with five other women, including Herlinda, I report each day to the small room at the end of A Hall on the first floor. We are employed by Federal Prison Industries, Inc. (trade name UNICOR) a "wholly owned, self-supporting Government corporation" that "maintains 80 industrial operations in 37 institutions, providing goods and services for sale to Federal Agencies." Monday through Friday, from nine to eleven A.M. and again from noon to four P.M., I think of myself not as a prisoner or a lunatic, but as an employee of the United States Postal Service. I imagine the Lonely Letter Carrier, trudging through rain, macing vicious suburban German shepherds, dropping envelopes decorated with the even-teethed smile of Ed McMahon into mailboxes across the land. Those envelopes, perhaps even one with the winning numbers enclosed, at some point in their journey may have been bundled into a maroon canvas bag that I had a hand in finishing. I wonder at the sense of pride this gives me, the sense that I am, though locked away, still somehow contributing.

The job itself requires no concentration. I remove a stack of stiff canvas bags from the trolley wheeled into the room each day by ancient Officer Svejk, an alarmingly thin hack with a glass eye who stands watch over us as we lace the bags. When I asked him how he wound up assigned here, he said, "Why, girlie, I'm just riding the old gravy train toward the retirement home. I'd rather spin it out in a basement full of loonies than over in the main compound. Ain't nearly so much conniving in here." Another day he told me that the thing he likes best about crazies is their honesty. I feel duty bound to lie to him.

I remove the bags in stacks of twenty, lug them to my place at the long table against the wall and seat myself on a stool between Herlinda and Lu Ng, a Vietnamese woman who cheated the Welfare Department. Dr. Hoffman says that Lulu has a neurological problem, not a mental one, because she was struck in the head by the butt of a rifle, courtesy of the 25th Infantry Division. Although I'm convinced that the neurological problem is real (headaches of six years' duration, occasional vertigo, weakness of the right limbs and blurred vision for the same period of time), I don't think it precludes mental-emotional disturbance.

On the table are ropes of clothesline, already cut and bundled, also in twenties. Next to that is a pile of metal clamps and next to that a pile of what look like metal shavings. These are made of something that weighs like aluminum but smells like nickel.

I pick up a length of rope and push it through the holes at the top of the mailbag — in one hole, out the other, in one hole, out the other — pull the ends of the rope even and thread them through the openings on a clamp before using a special kind of pliers to crimp the bits of metal onto the looped ends of the rope. And then I do it again.

Dr. Hoffman feels that a work routine will benefit Lulu; otherwise he would leave her free to wander the unit each day, as do Glenda, Nina and Three Sheets. I'm not at all certain that I agree with this course of therapy, though I know in my own case it is just what I need. Lulu, however, frequently misses a hole or two in the threading process; many of her bags are defective.

The stools they provide us with are too tall for the table, and by the time I've done eight or ten bags I feel my spine complaining, ranting about assembly line workers, Detroit, Chinese women in lower Manhattan, piecework, meat cutters, eight hours a day screwing bolt after bolt into barbecue grill after barbecue grill, about the massive backbreaking, all the sweat that pours so we can have the latest, newest, most improved antiperspirant, about the millions who leave work at five to go home and check the mailbox for a letter from Ed that says, *You may already be a winner.*

But I don't let minor physical discomforts or occasional attitude lapses interfere. I sit up straight and make one dollar and fourteen cents for every hundred bags I finish. My average is a hundred and eighty a day — a little more than two dollars and five cents for my labors. The money goes directly into my commissary account, and I am permitted to make purchases against my earnings. At present, because my status is "confined to unit," I deliver a list to whoever's on duty each Thursday and my shopping is done for me. Some of the women are allowed to walk, single file, under guard, down the wide corridor that leads to the main compound and the commissary, where they shop in person.

Though Nina says it's almost as much fun as going to the mall, I don't mind having to stay inside. I've been told that if there is a balance in my account on the date of my release, I may expect a government check within six to eight weeks of my discharge back into the real world. I have vowed to keep my purchases to a minimum, not to squander my earnings on candy bars and ice cream.

It isn't the money, obviously, that drives me to work so quickly and efficiently. Most of the women who work here on One finish around a hundred bags a day. I am productive beyond the Bureau of Prisons' wildest dreams. I do this to prove that I am stable, employable, reliable and earnest. If only the doctor would endorse my claim of sanity, I could take my case to a jury and once again become a contributing member of society. Of course, there's the possibility the jury might find me guilty. But I'm getting ahead of myself.

Doing the bags has become almost automatic, even though I've been less than a month on the job. When I wish to, I can sit here and let my hands work and think about other things. Often I choose to concentrate on what my hands are doing. Though I'm relatively new and almost certainly temporary, I have decided already that the Federal Bureau of Prisons does an admirable job of dealing with closed systems by assigning numbers, even here in the women's psychiatric unit. They have tempered the institutional nature of the place by naming it Veritas. It is a beautiful name, I think, subtly appropriate, best heard as a whisper.

Within the walls of my room are a stainless steel locker, a stainless steel sink-toilet combination and two beds. All of these are numbered. The gray metal stand next to my bed has an engraved aluminum plate attached to its left rear leg. Government issue, therefore numbered and periodically accounted for. There is crisscross green wire over the window, which looks out onto a courtyard formed on three sides by the red brick walls of this hospital. The fourth is a thick wall of the same brick topped off with chain link and concertina wire. Nina is fond of saying that it looks like a goddam war zone around here. She is 00926–086, I am 00917–088. Nina fights it, reversing or inserting digits whenever she must put her number on a form. I haven't yet told her how much I cherish mine.

I do not know my roommate's number; we are not that well acquainted. Her name is Emma, and before Dr. Hoffman assigned me to 304, he took me aside and asked me to keep a close eye on her, to call for help if I thought she might be about to make an attempt. I was reluctant at first to share a room with someone who was suicidal, but realized that doing so might help me prove myself to the doctor. I must move carefully, for if I make myself too valuable to him, he may attempt to keep me here regardless of whether I convince him I am competent. That is one of my most recently acquired fears.

It was during the so-called intake interview that Dr. Hoffman first put the idea in my mind. He was efficient that day; I was still in a state of shock, or something close to it, having been just delivered to this place by the marshals who took me from the courtroom. I was put in a room. I was left alone in the room for what seemed a long time, although I'm not sure, in clock time, exactly how long it was. I remember that it was cold; I remember feeling alone, feeling myself the only living presence in that room. And feeling precisely how cold it was, though it was April in Texas, and certainly warm outside. Outside there were clouds, and I was alert, aware of my body being in that place, that room, as though I were standing in a corner looking at myself perched on the edge of the chair, alone and frightened. After however long it was, Dr. Hoffman walked in and put a brief-case on the table between us. There was one other chair. Otherwise, the room was bare. He opened the case, removed some files, looked through them, pulled one out and spread its contents on the table. He took a pen from inside his navy sportcoat. It wasn't so much that I disliked him as that I thought it would be impossible for me to like anyone who occupied his position.

"Why did you do it?" he asked. "Did you think you were God?"

I was taken aback, more than taken aback. I was astonished. Afraid of my own anger. I said nothing. He stared at me.

"Name?"

"Cynthia Mitchell."

"Date of birth?"

"August 9, 1954."

"Place?"

"Fort Worth, Texas."

"You lived here then," he said. "Before. You lived here?"

"In Rancho Milagro. North of here."

Did I think I was God?

"Doctor," I ventured, "don't you already have all this information? I mean, I've given it to the police, the federal officers, the court, the marshals. I've told each of them. Is this interview necessary?"

"Not very much is," he said. "But if it makes you uncomfortable I can have my secretary take care of it. I sometimes find, though, that it helps, shall we say, to break the ice."

"I'm sorry," I said. "I am trying to be cooperative, but I

am exhausted. I cannot tell you how tired I am. I don't remember the last time I slept."

"Understandable," he said. "Were you employed?"

"When? I've been employed all my life."

"Prior to the — immediately prior to the incident."

"I was freelancing for a public relations firm."

"What did that involve?"

"I conducted focus groups. I ghost-wrote or edited articles for doctors who couldn't."

"Couldn't what?"

"Write."

"Foreign nationals, you mean."

"Most of them were Americans."

"What kind of papers?"

"Journal articles, mostly. In praise of some new drug or another."

"I can't say I read them. I find them tedious."

"As do I."

"Mrs. Mitchell, do you know why you're here?"

"I am here so that you can find me competent to stand trial. Is there any doubt in your mind, doctor, that I am competent?"

He began putting folders back in his briefcase.

"There is a great deal of doubt," he replied. "But that's why I'm here. To determine if you should be."

"Here? I don't think so."

"Well, then," he said, "at least one of us is certain. Actually, you should be glad you're here and not in some hellish state prison somewhere. It was smart of you to do him in on federal property. You're fortunate to have landed here. They say it's a country club, compared to most. Have you ever been in treatment? Any therapy?"

"No."

"Wonderful," he said.

I wasn't sure how to take his reaction. I wasn't sure of anything, except that I needed to close my eyes. I answered his questions the best I could.

"Yes," I responded. "No," I responded. "I don't know," I responded. It seemed to take hours. "Not lapsed, doctor," I responded. "Failed. I am a failed Catholic."

"Why such negativity?"

"That's a matter of opinion," I said.

I haven't learned much more about him in these intervening weeks, days, hours, minutes, et cetera. I've not learned much about anything. A little of this and a little of that about the women with whom I'm locked up. Et cetera. That time is passing is the only thing of which I'm certain.

Though I don't yet know Emma, my roommate, I have learned her routine. Every night, except Sundays, she sits cross-legged in the middle of her bed and makes paddling motions with her arms. "We are floating," she says always, "on the Sea of Compliance. Start rowing." She doesn't seem to mind when I pull the covers over my head.

On Sunday evenings she goes to the dayroom on Two and listens to Coffee recite. Coffee is in for armed robbery, and this is reflected in her poems. She is sometimes hostile. Dr. Hoffman has placed a video camera in the dayroom and given her permission to use it. So, once a week, while most of the inmate-patients are in the dayroom on Three watching something, Emma sits in a corner of the dayroom on Two while Coffee reads her poems into the vacant gray-black eye of the camera. Dr. Hoffman views the videos at his convenience. I hope one day to ask him if I may try my hand. He has not yet scheduled me for any tests. He is, he says, simply observing.

I am trying hard to adjust to my environment. Lights out is at ten, and Harold, looking more simian each time I see him, lopes in precisely on the hour to chase us from the dayroom. On Sundays, Coffee stands up to him quietly, removing her tape from the camera and handing it over with a dignity that forces him into a silent acknowledgment of her oppression.

Nights are difficult, tonight more than most. Beneath the blanket, I smell the saltiness of my own tepid breath and press my eyelids to keep the spiders out.

Today while I was at work, Coffee stole my wedding band. I'm sure of this. I thought I had it sufficiently hidden, tucked away in a bottle of moisturizer in the metal nightstand next to my bed.

I saw her eyeing it the first night I was in Veritas, when she stood in the doorway of 304 telling me she was afraid to come in because I had wicked-evil eyes. I assured her that was only because I'd seen some things. I sensed immediately that she would steal the ring, and forgave her instantly, before she was even fully aware of her decision to thieve from me. She left my watch, as I knew she would, and this reassures me. When I try to sleep, I hold my watch tightly in my left hand. The manufacturer has guaranteed that it is accurate to within three one-hundredths of a second per year.

Though I find it difficult to admit, I had grown fond of my wedding band. It was heavy, and of hammered gold, as was the afternoon of the ceremony. I will miss it even though my marriage was less than successful. My husband has been dead for just over a month now.

But I am sincere when I hope that the wedding band will bring Coffee some kind of pleasure. This should help me fall asleep, though tomorrow I will have to make a complaint. I don't want to; the idea of involving the authorities is wretched. Yet Coffee expects it of me; I must do it for her. She longs to lean against the wall with a smile on her lips and my wedding band up her ass while the hacks tear her room apart. Her gleeful anticipation demands that I report the theft. I know that it will be inconvenient for the rest of the inmates, including me, because the hacks will destroy our rooms when they conduct the search. Emma will be distraught when they rip the bedclothes from her personal *Narrenschiff,* her very own Ship of Fools, and toss them onto the floor. I will have to stand next to her, in the place just to the left of the green-painted doorframe where we are required to stand each afternoon for the four o'clock count, and assure her that she is not drowning. The count is important. We must all be here. I try to pay close attention. I urge myself to *Be Here Now,* to witness the event fully, even to the point of witnessing my own participation. I have learned to be both within myself and outside myself in these moments, but no one could tell just by looking.

Every day at four, weekends included, every single federal prisoner in every single federal prison is counted and accounted for. Down to the last. One by one the prisons call in their counts to the bureau headquarters in Washington. Only after each and every prisoner here and all of those out on the main compound are known to be present is the institutional all clear sounded. Then, unit by unit, we are released for evening chow. Unless, like those of us here in

Veritas, we happen to be in a special unit, where only the few who have been declared semifit by Dr. Hoffman are permitted onto the compound for meals. Most of us will stay locked where we are. Emma and I will stay. And Coffee and Nina and Three Sheets. Herlinda and her minions. Most of us.

Perhaps, while the hacks are counting, I should stand close to Emma and whisper to her that she must keep her knees slightly bent. Although Nina thinks it's only the secret to being a lady, I know better. Locked knees interfere with the circulation of the blood, trapping it in the lower extremities. By keeping the knees slightly bent, one may avoid fainting.

2 The voice coming from the window ledge sounds like bone being ground, and I cannot make out the words. When I open my eyes I am stunned to realize that I am still locked away in Veritas. I look to my right but see only hundreds of tiny diamonds of color, glittering at me from where the window should be.

I force myself to look past the green wire mesh, to concentrate on the sky, the clouds, the sun, to bring into focus those cosmic elements shared with the world outside these walls, shared even with the cemetery where the body of my husband, Daniel, lies.

There are odd moments when I miss him terribly, or miss my own idea of who or what he was. Yet even while I miss him I wonder to what degree my memory, which feels sometimes like guilt, is distorting the past. The early times especially. I can close my eyes and he is still with me, we are back on our first date, dinner at the Great Shanghai restaurant, and afterward, walking the small winding streets of Chinatown. He points out an arcade, closed for the night, with a sign out front: SEE THE DANCING CHICKEN! 25¢.

"What a poor brainless little thing it must be," he says, "spending its days dancing, wishing all the while it was sitting on a nest of eggs." He takes my hand as we walk toward Canal Street. "Think of it," he says, smiling. "I read this somewhere, incredible, that there are around thirty million hens in this country alone who are busting their asses every single day to produce enough eggs for America. Think of it. Clucking and squawking and laying those eggs, only to have them disappear onto a conveyor belt. Thirty million hens, robbed daily of their young, so we humans can dream up a hundred different ways to cook them. On that subject, would you consider having brunch with me tomorrow? My flight's not until four."

I decline but ask for a raincheck. He hails a taxi and rides with me to Eighty-eighth Street, sees me to my door and kisses me ever so gently before writing my phone number on the palm of his hand.

"I'll call and let you know when I'll be in town again," he says. "Soon. I know it'll be soon."

We will take our time, get to know each other slowly, see what happens. It has been one of those rare serendipitous evenings. I was a last-minute stand-in for a blind date whose feet got cold. A friend of sorts, more actually an associate at work, barged into my office at a quarter of six and pleaded with me to fill in for the date he'd set up for a pilot friend in town on an overnight.

I'd had misgivings about the pilot part.

"Please," he said. "Please please please. I beg a boon of thee. I'll do anything. Just go out with this guy. You'll like him. He's nice."

"But?"

"But what?"

"Finish your sentence. He's nice but . . ."

"But nothing. He's nice. He's fun to be with. I think you two would get along. He's from Texas. Aren't you from Texas? I thought you were from Texas."

"Previous life," I said. But I was intrigued. I wondered what it would be like to spend an evening with someone from "back home." It might be interesting, after all these years, to take a look at my home state through the eyes of a stranger.

And the evening was good. I enjoyed his company, the conversation; I liked him. I liked the intensity of his green eyes and the strength behind the gentleness in his hands.

I let myself into my apartment, still amused at the thought that I might be getting involved with a flyboy. But he had none of that cockiness which so many of them seem to have. When I'd asked what he did for a living, he said, "For a living, I do what bus drivers do, only I do it at around thirty-seven thousand feet. For pleasure, I do it closer to the ground, and in a much smaller plane. I'd love to take you up sometime. I promise no loop-the-loops."

The noise comes again, drawing me back to Veritas, drawing my eyes to a grackle that sits plumply on the window ledge, staring at me through the wire. Its feathers are so black and slick that the early sunlight makes them glint blue and green, turquoise and pink. The bird sees me watching and lets itself fall from the ledge, swooping gracefully, almost glancing across the athletic green pavement of the courtyard before it arcs skyward and sails over the concertina wire atop the wall.

Emma sleeps crumpled on a bare mattress. Her pillow, caseless, is on the floor, and sometime during the night she has pushed her woolen army blanket down into the space between the mattress and the gray metal frame that holds it. She refused to remake her bed after the hacks finished looking for my ring. "I will wait until Friday," she told me. Friday is laundry day, when we turn in our bedclothes and are issued washed sheets. She was angry at me because the hacks found her stash of Tawny Bisque Cover Girl. Cosmetics, like matches and chewing gum, are forbidden.

Except for her face, Emma is pale when awake, and in sleep her skin goes so white that I must listen for the short, light sounds of her breathing to make sure she is still alive. Her body is bone thin, so light that it doesn't make an impression in the mattress, and her cheeks and chin are scorched pink from the medicine Dr. Hoffman has prescribed. She has deforming acne and believes it is a symptom of something gone wrong within, a physical manifestation of a defect in her soul.

I'm not sure how to convince her otherwise. It is all I can do to get her to look at me. Her locker is full of *Vogue*s and *Cosmo*s, stacked almost four feet deep. Before she throws one out or leaves it in the dayroom for others to snatch, she finds the page with the photo of what she thinks is the most beautiful woman in the issue, tears it out and puts it in a manila folder that she begged from Dr. Hoffman. She did not allow me to see it for quite some time, but then one night, well after lights out, after she had rowed her bed over the Sea of Compliance and fallen forward, exhausted, she dragged herself to her locker and brought out the folder. On the cover, printed in careful block letters, were the words WHAT I'M NOT.

She held it out to me and said, "Just look at these."

I tried to point out to her the freakish nature of the cover girls' features, the emaciation of their bodies, tried to show her where noses had been spliced, chins sculpted, breasts enlarged, thighs suctioned.

"They're perfect," she said, "beautiful and perfect."

"Emma," I said, "look closely. They're freaks. And they're airbrushed. They're not real."

She took the folder from me silently and returned it to her locker, and refused to speak to me for days. She rowed silently each night, staring at the wall in front of her, unwilling even to glance in my direction.

Before I reported my wedding band missing, I told her, as I told everyone I could find, that there would be a search. But for some reason she did not try to hide her contraband.

Nina, as always, took immediate action; she stole a roll of tape from Dr. Hoffman's office and secured her bag of pills beneath one of the bathroom sinks several hours before the hacks began ransacking the unit.

Coffee has her first real audience. Emma is here, faithful as ever, but Herlinda has come too and brought her clique of six Cubans, whose names I do not know. Nina has come, and even Three Sheets, who stands, redheaded, in a corner, swaying to the rhythm of her medication. Coffee is loading the tape into the camera when Glenda walks in, trailing scarves from her wrists.

"Janna wants you to know she would be here if she could," Glenda says, and sits down on the orange vinyl couch behind the camera. Janna is locked in 309, the room directly across from mine. I've glimpsed her, but Dr. Hoffman has forbidden anyone to talk to her, and she's never even come to her window that I know of. They have her on twenty-three-hour lockdown. Once a day a hack takes her out for what they call recreation. Usually she spends her hour in the courtyard, bouncing a handball against the wall.

Coffee takes her place in front of the camera, holding a single piece of paper, which she looks at for a moment before crumpling it and throwing it to the floor.

"Okay," she says, and Emma rises to press a button on the camera.

"May 8, 1988, eight-twelve P.M.," Coffee says. "Thank you all for being here, and happy Mother's Day to all the mothers."

Everyone looks around, waiting for someone to take credit. Finally Herlinda says thank you. Coffee cocks one hip and slices the air with a flat hand, waist high.

"This is called 'Even,' " she says.

We rolled into East Saint Louie like a funnel cloud
low hanging and
full of threatening silence.
Cased a place
or two or three
Decided on one for the robbery.
(Tell the boys on Wall Street we got
almost a hundred even.)

Not even enough
to get off
real good again.
Not even enough for a buzz.
Go on, tell the white boys about it. Tell 'em!
Tell *all* the white boys.
Tell them in their pretty white shirts
with their pretty red ties
and their lovely white wives
and their black motherfucking
cash-filled attaché *cases.*
We got almost a hundred even.
But not even.

Coffee takes her eyes from the camera and glares around the room, stands there daring. Nobody says anything, and then Nina shifts her bathrobe around and pulls out a cigarette, nudging Herlinda for a match.

"Girlfriend," she says, "if you're letting Dr. H listen to that shit I hope you got stock in Sony, 'cause your ass is gonna be videotaping for another ten years easy."

"What I want to know," Coffee says, "is did it give you something."

"Jesus, Mary and Joseph, Coffee," Herlinda says, "write something pretty, write something hopeful or . . . or write *anything,* but don't let him see that."

"Yeah," Nina says, "write something nice. You might be able to cop some cash from the NEA." She tries to pocket Herlinda's matches but gets caught.

"I'm asking you if you *got* anything from it," Coffee says. "I don't give a midday shit about what Hoffman thinks. He's the whitest man on the planet. Now, answer. What'd you get from it."

Nina is rolling through the stairwell doors as she calls out over her shoulder, "What I got from it, *Mizz Thing*, is one bad motherfucking headache. Later, ladies."

We sit quietly, Herlinda fingering her matchbook, while Emma rewinds the videotape. Coffee stands alone in the middle of the room, but she has gone far away from us; she is seeing something different from the beige floor tile at which she stares.

Minutes pass, keep passing. I don't know if they are going quickly or slowly, only that they are going steadily. That is enough. They are accumulating: the space between Daniel's death and my own present is expanding, growing ever larger, filling with time.

There were times when I thought that I could not live without him, that if something happened to him I would voluntarily follow. But he is gone, and here I am.

From the first, we loved the outdoors together. There was the week we spent on Saint John Island, the sun gloriously warm on our shoulders. On an early morning when the air was still fresh with the memory of night, we drove our rented jeep along the winding tree-shaded blacktop to a wide shoulder near the start of the trail, parked and let ourselves into the forest. A young family, father, son and daughter anyway, was just coming back up the trail as we entered. They wished us good morning and the little girl squealed happily as her dad whooshed her into the air and helped her scramble up the embankment to the roadway. After that, we saw no one.

There was a mood to the forest, tropical, rich with oxygen; it seemed itself to have the heart of one animal, to take deep easy breaths while it watched us on the trail, surrounded us, welcomed us into its ancient and mystical rhythms.

Daniel and I went silently, enchanted by the huge trees, hearing the calls of birds and the sound of our own soft footfalls on the earth. He walked ahead of me for a while, until we saw that the trail, though narrow, was reliable and easily navigated. Then he stepped back and smiled, open and warm, as I passed.

We had gone for some time when he called out to me. I backtracked the few yards to where he stood staring up at the top of a tree.

"It looks like a giant nest of dirt daubers," he said, pointing to a large clump of black that hung like rotting fruit speared in a fork of the tree's branches. "But look." His finger followed several thin trails of black that came out of the clump and dribbled down the tree trunk and into the earth, looking like an army of tiny black ants trailing its way willy-nilly down the trunk from the fruit.

A small placard at the base of the tree identified the growth as a member of the Clusia family, commonly called the strangler fig. A parasite, it would take up residence at the bottom of a host tree and grow its way up the trunk, then lodge in the branches and begin sending out tendrils that would grow back down and gradually encircle the trunk, attempting, and often succeeding, in choking its host to death.

Now that we knew to look for them, we saw the strangler figs everywhere; the forest was occupied by them. The placard said that it might take twenty years or longer for the parasite to kill its host or succumb itself. We were fascinated, Daniel especially. There, in what we thought was the blissful peace and quiet of a glorious tropical morning, we were surrounded by plants locked in silent, mortal combat.

Something bumps my shoulder, pulling me back to the dayroom.

". . . yeah, you," Herlinda is saying, "you, whitegirl, gringa, where'd you go? You know they'll add five *años* to your sentence if you escape. Tell us where did you go? Where did you escape to?"

I look hard at her for a moment, stretching the silence only because I realize I must. I don't want confrontation. But if I give in to her too quickly, she will attempt to force her will upon me, she will seek to show the others that the newcomer is weak before her established power. I remember what Coffee said about my eyes being wicked-evil, and although I am sure they are not, I know I can use them to my advantage. My eyes will say things so that my voice doesn't have to.

Tuesday's lunch hour is almost over, and I should go back to work, but I am enjoying the dance. I often find myself without appetite until dinner, so at lunchtime I take only a roll and a glass of whatever color Kool-Aid is being offered. This leaves me with almost forty-five minutes to spend alone in my room, and on Tuesdays and Thursdays I can look down from my window and watch Glenda bounding about in the courtyard, lost in her afternoon scarf dance. She does this regularly, immediately following her appointments with Dr. Hoffman. When the weather is bad she dances indoors, in the dayroom, but when the afternoons are warm she takes herself outside.

I don't know where she gets the scarves, but I'm told they change monthly. For May she has yellow and green chiffons, long ones, which she twirls and snaps in the air around her head. She is slender and wears toe shoes with her cutoffs and bikini top. The shoes, too, are replaced often. The concrete courtyard tends to shred the delicate pink fabric.

Glenda started doing dead time about eight months ago, when she declared to Dr. Hoffman that she was in tune with the cosmic consciousness and that she had only goodness within her. The doctor wasted no time in slapping her with the incompetent label, stopping her clock at three years, four months. She had only fourteen months left on her sentence, but until he decides that she knows she's in prison, days served don't count. I think of Glenda as having achieved a state of grace, but Dr. Hoffman has more than once referred to her as his Pretty Jung Thing. She certainly dances beautifully and does not seem bothered by Dr. Hoffman's decision. She recently discovered that the beauty marks on her left forearm form a human-scale Capricorn, and is determined to raise the rest of the zodiacal constellations on her body by sunning herself during the appropriate months.

Today her tape player blares rock, a favorite among us inmates, the Archetypal Vaginas singing "Dentata." Glenda seems to have energy enough to do a few good leaps. Some days she just stands out there, dropping the scarves and picking them up, dropping the scarves and picking them up. Herlinda says that when Glenda has a bad day, you can expect rain. When I asked her how long they can keep Glenda here, she let out a slow sigh and said, "Forever, gringa, forever." No one seems to know why she is here, not even Nina.

I met Glenda my first day in, when I walked into the lavatory and she began screaming and threw a bar of soap at me. The hacks came running and escorted me to the facilities on Two. When Glenda is in the bathtub, no one is allowed to enter. She puts a hot oil treatment into her waist-length black hair and wraps her head in plastic, leaving it for the duration of her bath, which can take from thirty minutes to as long as an hour and a half. As far as I know she gets violent only when interrupted during ablutions. Yesterday, Three Sheets managed to intrude and was struck with a wooden scrub brush, but took no offense, only smiling while a huge red welt rose up on her wide and idle forehead. When the hacks came to lead her away, Glenda shrieked out after her, "Stealing is bad karma, Three Sheets!"

But today she twirls giddily, lacing the air with yellow and green, her body pretzeling gently to the music. The courtyard creates a slight echo, but Glenda maintains step to the distorted music even when it doubles back on itself after hitting the walls. I watch until I am thoroughly late for work.

As I leave my room, Janna hisses at me through the window in her door. I'm not sure what she wants, but when she sticks an index finger through a diamond of wire and beckons, I walk over. Her room is identical with the one I'm assigned, but there is only one bed. She has a stack of hardcovers on her windowsill. I notice *The Seven Pillars of Wisdom*.

"Who are you?" she asks. Her T-shirt is stained on the front with something blueberryish, purple, in the shape of a handprint, and her eyes are almost the same shade. She has on wheat-colored jeans that hang loose on her hips and her brown hair is practically crewcut. She looks about twelve.

"My name is Cynthia."

"I'm Janna," she says. "They won't let me out of here

because they say I'm *aggressive*. Like, uncontrollable. Yeah-right. The thing is, I shouldn't even be here, I should be at Alderson uh-cause I'm a juvie, seventeen, but the buttholes there say I have to have a fucking psychiatric evaluation so they ship my ass up here and I can *not* get them to let me out of this fucking room for love or money. I did robberies. What did you do?"

I look at my watch and tell her I'm late for work.

"Okay-yeah," she says, "whatever. Later, man."

As I turn away I notice that she has tied the cord of the venetian blinds on her window into a neat, miniature hangman's noose.

This morning at eleven when they rolled the stainless steel lunch cart with its rows of red plastic trays and its pliable white plastic cutlery into the kitchen, I had done fewer than my requisite sixty mailbags. I hurried to finish some more before Officer Svejk herded us out of the work-room, but in the end came up short. And now I am late returning. I scold myself for daydreaming about Glenda, for wishing that it were I instead of she dancing in the court-yard. I lament Janna's decision to break her monumental silence just at the end of my lunch hour. I make my hands move faster. Herlinda leans over and whispers, "Lay off, gringa, you make too much work." I ignore her. I whip the ropes through the openings and try not to think. I am a machine, an assembly line in and of myself. My hands fly.

"Gringa," Herlinda whispers, "I mean it. Lay off a little bit, will you?"

"Herlinda," I answer grimly, "you do what works for you. Let me do what I have to."

"You don't have to make the rest of us look like such slowpokes," she says.

"I'm not making you look like anything. I'm just trying to get caught up. I've been behind all day."

"Like another six cents at the end of the month is gonna buy you a new life? I say give it a rest, whitegirl."

"I'm only going for two hundred."

"Oh. Only two hundred. Tell me, did you, when you were on the outside, did you, were you one of those ones who like work like all the fucking time? Are you like one of those who live to work?"

"Hardly." She can't possibly understand. None of them can possibly understand. I'm not working so hard. I'm managing. I know how to concentrate. I know how not to think about the things I shouldn't. Concentration takes me outside this place. The only thing I have to watch out for is that my eyes don't get confused. Sometimes my hands move so fast they almost seem to take on the color of the canvas mailbags. They turn a dark red, almost maroon, and it becomes hard to see where they are or what they're doing. I try not to let it disturb me.

But I can see Officer Svejk, standing at the edge of my vision, lighting his umpteenth cigarette of the day and staring at me through the smoke as though he thinks I've gone mad. If only they would let me, I'm certain I could keep the entire U.S. Postal Service supplied with mailbags. I crimp with a vengeance.

3

The sound of shattering glass, when I happen to hear it, always reminds me of Daniel. The noise itself is unsettling, rattling the tiny delicate bones of the middle ear, and remembrances of my husband are even harsher. I am still at the point where it takes me a few static-filled seconds after thinking of him to remember that he's dead.

It is this which yanks me from sleep, and I am sitting before I am awake, wondering whether it was part of a dream or real. The hall is quiet.

Then more glass, more breaking. Not a dream. I tell myself to stay quiet; I lie down and pull the covers to my chin. Emma rests on, slumbering behind whatever pill Dr. Hoffman gave her after dinner. When she has spent a sufficient number of hours in tears, Dr. H takes pity and plays the role of the Sandman. I've been unable to cry since Daniel's funeral, and I worry that this is a symptom of maladjustment.

Down the hall comes the squish-soft tread of the night hack, a nurse named Mrs. Palazzetti. She stops at 309 and I hear her scratchy red voice croak out, "There now, Janna, what are you doing."

Something slams against a wall; something sounds like books being thrown on the floor. I hear Janna grunting with rage as she picks up the end of her bed and drops it, picks it up and drops it.

"Janna," Mrs. Palazzetti says, "you know I'll have to get the guards, I'll have to get Dr. Hoffman."

"GET THEM!" Janna screams. "GET THEM AND GET DR. MOTHERFUCKINGDOGASS HOFFMAN TOO. I WANT OUT OF HERE AND I WANT OUT NOW." Her voice is animal bellow, hitting like a fist to the face, leaving me breathless and shaking, afraid to move, and ashamed that I am unwilling to do so.

Mrs. Palazzetti hits the red body alarm she wears on her waist and charges back down the hall. I focus on the soft *pffts* of air that slip from her cushioned soles each time one of them strikes the tile; it's so quiet I can even hear the swoosh-rub of the nylon coating her thighs. Then the whump of the door shutting, and the hall is still with anticipation, full of listening inmates.

A draft of cool air flows under the door, Emma sleeps, I climb out of bed and feel the cold linoleum through my socks as I slip toward the door. Janna stands on her bed. Through her window and mine I can see waist to shoulder. She is holding her bloody right fist with her bloody left hand. She has put two holes in her window, one dead center, the other above it and to the left.

"Fifty-seven fucking days," she screams. "Fifty-mother-fucking-seven days I've been in this room! I have my rights. You can't do this to me. I have my rights. I want out. Out-out-out-out-out. GET MY ASS OUT OF HERE! Get me out-OUT-OUT-OUT-OUT," she barks. "AH-OOOOOWT," she is howling. "OUT-out-out-out-out-OUT!" she levels it into a nightmare moan aimed with deadly futile accuracy at the indifference of her surroundings. "BITCHES!" she screams. "All you worthless fucking bitches on this hallway, why won't you help me? Somebody help me!"

Someone begins chirping like a bird.

Keys jangle down the hall, mensteps, forceful and heavy. Behind them, wheezing with the effort of keeping up, Mrs. Palazzetti. I step back from my door into darkness as the lead hack punches his key into Janna's door lock. They have her out in no time, strong-arming her down the hall, leaving behind the echo of her shouts and a trail of blood spots.

Mrs. Palazzetti turns off the light in Janna's room and pulls the door shut. I walk over and slip a finger beneath Emma's nose, feel her warm breath fluttering against my knuckles.

I realize I'm shivering and get back into bed. I lie quietly, feeling the glass and metal of my wristwatch warming against the skin of my palm, and finally the chirping stops. For some reason I think it was Three Sheets, though I've never heard her utter a sound.

I know I won't be able to fall asleep soon, but I close my

eyes anyway, massaging my scalp around the ears to try to erase Janna's sounds. I'm sure her fist will need stitches.

When I went to view Daniel, the first thing I noticed was the mortician's artful job of sewing him up. At the burial, I was in custody, and so watched from a distance. It seemed to me unusual that I'd been taken there. I thought for a while it was kindness, but then realized the authorities were hoping to jar me into a confession. I remember handcuffs. I remember being glad there were so many trees in the graveyard. His family said nothing to me as they walked along the gravel path to their cars when the burial was done.

Enough, I tell myself. Don't succumb. Enough. I will not lie here digging up the pain, turning it over like garden soil, hoping absurdly that something green and beautiful and living might sprout from it.

Mrs. Palazzetti has her feet up, watching the movie with the rest of us. Except for the light from the TV, the dayroom is dark. I have grown fond of the ubiquitous bubbas who stride manfully across the tube through huge parking lots of gleaming used cars, slapping fenders affectionately and urging me to come on down for the bestest deals of my cotton-picking life. But there are evenings when the dayroom is noisy enough to chase me away to the solitude of my room. Coffee likes to scream obscenities at Dan Rather. Nina is an ace at "Jeopardy!" And the babble during "Wheel of Fortune" is sometimes unbearable.

Tonight, though, is quiet, especially for a Saturday. The room is thick with lethargy, the only safe response to Janna's early morning violence — yet another instance of lassitude imitating sanity.

Nina and Lulu have brought their pillows along so they'll have something to hug while they watch *Holiday* (first teaming of Grant and Hepburn). The television is angled in the corner, aimed at the intersection of two long orange-vinyl couches that can only be described as bastardized Danish modern. There are plastic wood-grain coffee tables in front of each, and a corner table where they meet. Against the south wall are a couple of collapsible cafeteria tables and several folding metal chairs of assorted bright colors. The red one stays in the corner next to the stairwell door and is reserved for Three Sheets, the only concession she has demanded of anyone.

If it is possible, even Three Sheets is more subdued than usual tonight. Ordinarily, she never stays put in her chair for more than twenty or thirty seconds, though she does stop to sit down each time she happens to pass it. She's been there for almost thirty minutes now by my watch, since about the time Cary Grant floated into Nick and Susan's apartment and said, "It's love, fellas. I've met a girl." Coffee started to say something, but settled for punching the couch in the empty space next to her.

Katharine Hepburn is sitting in the playroom, saying, "You see, Case, the trouble with me is that I never could decide whether I wanted to be Joan of Arc, Florence Nightingale or John L. Lewis," when Herlinda tiptoes into the room with her coterie. They give Three Sheets wide berth as they whisper-giggle toward a vacant table. Herlinda gathers the women there and says something in Spanish before slinking over to sit between Nina and me.

When a commercial comes on I ask Herlinda why her gang is afraid of Three Sheets.

"They're not my gang," she says.

I apologize and she nods obstinately, tapping one finger against the heavy gold H that hangs from her left earlobe. Jewelry, like matches, chewing gum and cosmetics, is contraband. The exceptions are wedding rings and wristwatches, but for some reason Herlinda gets away with wearing half a dozen chains and assorted earrings. She says it is because she threatened to put spells on any hack who even thought about forcing her to comply with the regulation. It amuses her that the guards went for it.

"And they are not afraid of Three Sheets," she says.

"Why do they whisper about her?"

Herlinda rolls her eyes and sucks her teeth at me. "How do you know, my little gringa, that they are not whispering about you?"

"What is it they say?"

"*Quien mató a su hermana,*" Herlinda says softly.

"God," Nina drawls, "Saturday night and we're cooped up like hens, with not a red rooster in sight." She stuffs her chin into her pillow. "And it's hotter than the hinges of hell in this place. I'm soaked. Somebody turn up the AC."

When no one moves, Nina gets up and adjusts the thermostat herself, staring at the dial until the compressor comes on and cool air begins falling from the overhead vents.

Herlinda waits until Nina is comfortable again before saying, "Look over your shoulder, sweetheart." I watch Nina gaze toward the table full of Cuban women. Herlinda smiles. "See Louisa?" she questions. "In the yellow blouse? You could have some fun."

Nina shrinks around her pillow, pulling her exquisitely plucked blond eyebrows into a scribble.

"You're so bored," Herlinda says calmly. "And Louisa

likes you very much. Conchita will pin for you. Just for one pack of Marlboro Lights."

Nina sits calculating for a moment while Herlinda winks at Louisa.

"I can't pay you until next commissary day," Nina says.

"*Bueno*, then," Herlinda answers, and nods at Louisa.

The three of them wait until Mrs. Palazzetti's eyes droop before slipping out of the dayroom, which is filling now with conditioned air and the aura of conspiracy. We will all sit quietly, watching the movie, while Nina and Louisa go to Nina's bed and Conchita stands inconspicuously in the hallway, ready to explode in a loud fit of coughing if she sees a hack.

When she is on duty during the week, Mrs. Palazzetti is very prompt about lights out, but Saturdays she is just as reliable about dozing off during the movie. I don't think it's a case of fatigue; I think it is her way of being kind, telling us that there is someone willing to trust us, regardless.

I venture a quiet look around the room, not wanting to disturb the somnolence. Lit in television gray, the faces belong to strangers, women from all over the country. Most I know only from seeing them in the hall during the afternoon count. I watch them standing, leaning, slouching while one hack stays at the end of the hall and his partner marches, businesslike, his clear voice ringing, "One, two, three . . . eleven, twelve, thirteen. All here in A Hall," before they take their clipboards to B Hall and then downstairs to Two.

Janna is on Two now. Coffee says there are three women down there, and that Two is where Dr. Hoffman conducts serious therapy. Nina and Coffee have each given me an account of what really goes on down there, including the use of restraints, straitjackets and electroshock therapy. A Hall, which runs off the dayroom, is supposedly empty, though we have no way of knowing because the heavy doors stay locked and the window is papered over on the inside. I've tried to peek through while Coffee reads her poetry, but there is not so much as a pinhole in the paper. B Hall is the one in use, but we can't get any closer to it than the stairwell doors outside the dayroom at the opposite end of the unlabeled connecting hall. And the Control Room, where the hacks congregate, is just outside the door leading to B Hall.

I am afraid to think of Janna strapped to a bed while they send electricity through her body, and in the same instant doubt the legitimacy of my worry. I tell myself I am being absurdly sentimental, that Janna is none of my concern. We spoke only that one time. Still, I wish I could see for myself that she is all right.

Three Sheets stirs in her corner, stands and walks in several tight circles before sitting back down to study something invisible on her hands. Her slow rocking quickens until her agitation at whatever it is she thinks she is balancing on her thickly padded palms becomes worrisome. I fear she will wake Mrs. Palazzetti, so I go to her and pull up a chair.

She stops rocking and whips her eyes back and forth between my hands and her own. I reach slowly and take one of her wrists, rubbing her palm and then dusting it lightly before scooping air off and tossing it to the floor. She grinds her foot over the spot where whatever I threw down would have landed. She offers her other hand, and this too I clean. I sit for a moment longer while she forces the second demon into the floor.

She stands up and begins chirping happily, sounding like a songbird, although I haven't a clue which particular one she is imitating. She continues to sing softly as she sits down and begins her normal, slow rocking. When she looks as though she will stay quietly put, I make my escape.

I wander back to the couch confused, wondering whether I have just touched the hands of a murderer, and am relieved when Herlinda nudges me and nods in Mrs. Palazzetti's direction.

"Good move, gringa," she says. "I want so much to see the end of this flick."

"Herlinda," I whisper, "how long have you been here?"

"Let me see," she sighs. "It is fourteen months now."

"In the States, I mean."

"Since the boats," she says. She nods toward the table. "All of us together. Since Mariel."

Coffee rouses herself to glare from her place on the other couch.

"Hey," she whispers, "you bitches want to talk, go on down the hall. *Some* of us are trying to stay with the program here."

Herlinda looks at sleeping Mrs. Palazzetti, then at me, and shrugs. I follow the clinking of her jewelry down A Hall, past Conchita, past the towel hanging over the window of Nina's door and into 306.

"We're not supposed to congregate in the rooms," I say, knowing this would be only my first offense. I would get away with a warning, which is why I'm willing to risk it.

"Gringita," Herlinda laughs, "what are they going to do if they catch you? Put you in jail?"

Her room is a double, like mine and Emma's, but she has decorated carefully. Above the sink-toilet is a picture of a woman in a monk's robe wearing a necklace of pearls. Yellow light shines behind her.

"Pelagia the Penitent," Herlinda says. She reaches beneath her mattress and pulls out something that looks like an IUD with an electrical cord attached. "Would you like tea?"

"Thank you, yes," I say. She draws water from the sink into two polystyrene cups and holds the heating coil in the center of one. "It takes time," she says, "and you have to hold it or it will burn through the cup."

There are no green army blankets in this room. Instead, a crocheted comforter in bright reds, oranges and browns is arranged on one bed, and on the other, a creamy yellow lace spread. Above the window, long multicolored scarves are hung as bunting. A rosary, taped to the side of her locker, is draped in the form of a shield around five or six laminated holy cards. I don't know how so many inmates manage to smuggle in so many touches from home, but I'm glad they find ways to add to the charm of the unit décor. I don't plan to be here long enough to get comfortable.

"Your tea?"

I take the cup politely and do not complain to her that the water is lukewarm.

"Please," Herlinda says, "sit over there." She points to her roommate's bed and then settles herself carefully on her own. "Coffee says you are dangerous. I wonder why."

"Why you are here?"

"Why am I here? Because I came with the rest." She shudders. "In Cuba, we chopped cane. From sunup to sundown, chopping, all day long, chopping at sugar cane. I am sick even now when the smell comes to me. If you fall from the heat, they come at you with whips; when they get tired of whipping, they send the dogs." She sits staring into her cup while I wonder what to say.

"It is much better here." She smiles suddenly. "We sit at night, watch the TV, we have midnight tea. Three hots and a cot, isn't that it?" She raises her cup to me. "Why did you kill your sister?"

"Herlinda," I say quietly, "I did not kill my sister."

"But Louisa says it too. You killed your sister."

"That's what they think? It's not true. It's just not true. I worked in public relations."

"Calm down." She takes a slow sip of tea. "I believe you. What is public relations?"

"Promotions. We did promotions. Kind of like advertising. Our firm did mostly pharmaceuticals, medicines."

"Ahh, *los narcos!*"

"No," I say. "An evaluation, to determine whether or not I can stand trial. I shouldn't be here at all."

She smiles at this.

"Of course," she says. "None of us should be here. It's all a mistake."

"How can you sell your friends, Herlinda? How could you do that to Louisa? For a pack of cigarettes."

"It bothers you?"

"I guess it does. Yes. It makes me angry."

"Louisa isn't doing anything she doesn't want to do. You didn't see me offer any of the others, did you?"

"But to sell her? What does she get from it? She doesn't even smoke."

"The cigarettes are for me," she says. "Louisa speaks no English; none of them do. I take care of them. I have taken care of them since we came over. Believe me, I only offered Louisa because she told me she wanted it. I was doing

them a favor. Is your husband waiting for you, on the outside?"

"I'm not married."

"Then why the search for your wedding band?"

"I used to be married."

"You still love him?"

"He's dead."

"Do you still love him?"

"We had our differences."

"Give me, as you say, a yes or a no."

I feel myself shifting on the bed. "It was complicated."

"Oh, poor gringa," she says. She looks at me as she might
a child who has muddied a brand-new party dress. "I will
read the water for you."

"What?"

"The water," she says. "I can see the future in water,
like a crystal ball. But not tonight. It's late and I am out of
matches."

"Is there more tea?"

"Of course," she says, "but let's take it to the dayroom."

I follow her down the long hallway; the flickering gray-
white light from the dayroom carries me to the end of a
day-long snowstorm and the night Daniel took me to a wedding atop the World Trade Center. It was early, maybe our
fifth or sixth date. Friends of Daniel's; people I'd never even
met. Hundreds of people, smiling and well-wishing, dressed
to the nines. The ceremony was performed by a woman
judge. When violins sang the wedding march, the room
filled with one big hush of anticipation. I watched the
groom standing up front, waiting, hands clasped, looking for
all the world as though he were calm. The bride looked
startled that we all stood as she entered, but smiled, first
bravely, then genuinely, as only a bride can.

Daniel took my arm as we seated ourselves again.

"She's lovely," he said quietly. "They'll make a great couple." Then he slipped his hand from my arm and rested
it for just the slightest instant on my belly. "Hmmm,"
he whispered, "ever think about babies?" He squeezed my
hand and leaned back in his seat. Though his hand was
holding mine, I could feel it still on my belly, and though
I could not believe he had said what he just said, for the first
time in my life I seriously considered the possibility. A
baby. Children. A family.

The judge said, "I now pronounce you wife and husband," and we all applauded and smiled, and as the bride
and groom walked down the aisle I could feel the room
filling with good wishes for them, everyone sending them
hopes for a wonderful future. It was a tangible warmth, and
I found myself, though I hadn't met them, wishing them
all good things, health and happiness, as I stood holding
Daniel's hand.

Later, when we were dancing, he said we should think
about having an outdoor ceremony.

"Perhaps on the back lawn," he said. "Oh, but wait" —
he smiled suddenly — "you haven't asked me to marry you
yet, have you?" He pulled me close and we glided around
the floor, surrounded by dancing couples caught up in the
romance of the evening. "Better hurry," he said. "Unless of
course you expect me to do the asking."

Near the evening's end, we were standing at one of the
windows, a hundred and seven stories up, looking out over
New York and beyond, the glittering bridges, the thousands
of lit windows, the shimmering reflections in the river, the
harbor, everything brilliant in the icy January night air.

"I know you think I'm kidding," Daniel said. "Or else
you think I'm moving awfully fast." He took my left hand

and began playing with it, slipping a make-believe ring onto my finger. "But I'm not kidding. And I am moving fast. For the first time ever I know that I'm in love. You are the most wonderful woman I've ever met in my life, and I want you to be my wife."

He put a finger to my lips and shushed me when I started to answer. "Not yet," he said. "Don't answer yet. Think about it. Think about it and tell me when you're ready." He held his arm out to me and I slipped mine through it. "Let's go check out another view. I think from the other side we should be able to get a great look at the Statue of Liberty."

Something is at my shoulder. Herlinda.

"Cynthia," her mouth says. "What is the major malfunction, gringa?" The hallway looms; I follow her toward the dayroom. "Hurry," she says. "The flick must be almost over, and I like happy endings."

4

When I ask him for the razor, Harold, the testosterone king who torments Coffee every Sunday night, ignores me for a few moments. I stand silently, and finally he looks up from his sports page and says, "What's up? Got a date?"

"Yes," I say. "The Fort Worth Jaycees are dropping in for a buffet supper at nine. I think I'll wear my yellow chiffon."

I follow him as he slugs his way to the nurses' station on One and keys open the locker. Razors, obviously, are contraband. The one Harold hands me is old-fashioned, made of anodized brass with curved flaps that hinge open to take the double-edge blade when you turn the knob at the base of the handle. This one has been modified to require a small key for a lock set in the bottom of the knob. I know I'll feel compelled to remove the blade simply because they've taken steps to prevent my doing so. I envision myself in contraband heaven, standing in the shower, wearing loads of jewelry and waterproof mascara, chewing gum while I shave my legs and think about how to get the blade out. After all, I know how to handle sharp objects.

Wrist scars are common around here. Emma and Nina both have them, as do several others. Nina's run crosswise, like a bracelet. But Emma knew what she was doing, gouging in the direction of the slender tendon that runs just beneath the skin. The seamlike cicatrix of her attempt, puffy and pink on the blue-white tissue of her wrist, seems to me all too public a sign of what should be a very private penultimate failure.

I sign the book and ask Harold if I may stay on One for my shower. He scratches his whiskered jaw, looking doubtful.

"Harold," I say, "I just want a little privacy. Glenda is in the tub on Two, and Three is simply a madhouse."

"I want to see you upstairs in thirty minutes," he says, checking his watch. "Not a second after eight-fifteen."

"Thank you."

"I mean it," he says. "You're not there, I'm coming straight down here and dragging you out."

I take my time. The water is reassuring, something that has come from outside the compound. I soap myself slowly, wondering whether it's the shower's privacy or isolation that I want more. There are still moments when I wish for Daniel, forgetful moments tinted pink with optimistic nostalgia. The best kiss we ever shared was in a shower, in a house in Vermont where we were visiting friends. They'd gone out for the afternoon, leaving us surrounded by the quiet of deep green woods, and he was there that day. With me and gentle, his fingertips light on the back of my neck.

"I'm so glad I found you," he'd said. "I thank God every day that we met. And I can't wait until we have a baby."

I dry myself and take the razor to my room. Emma's bed is empty and I am grateful. I'm still not sure why I want the blade, but a simple pair of tweezers does the job beautifully. In no time at all the paper-thin, platinum-coated double-edge blade is resting on the palm of my hand, weightless. I stand and stare at it, wondering where to hide it, wondering whether I shouldn't just put it back in the razor. But there is something about the extent of their control over my life at this point that makes me want to get away with something, with anything, even something so foolish, so pointless, as this. I don't want the blade. I have no use for it. But they've gone to such lengths to prevent me from getting it that I feel the need to circumvent their precautions. I open my locker and dig through the magazines at the bottom. I am leafing through an old *Elle* when I hear Harold marching down the hall. I slip the blade behind a page showing a pair of gorgeous legs and a bottle of depilatory cream.

I have just got the razor closed when Harold bangs through the door.

"Give it up," he says.

"What," I say.

"You know," he answers. "Come on."

"I didn't realize I'd taken so long." I hand him the razor. "I'm sorry."

"You sure are," he deadpans, stuffing it in the back pocket of his dirty white pants. "Trust you people and what happens."

I listen as he grumbles down the hall, waiting for him to discover the missing blade and run back yelling, but all I hear is Nina saying, "Hey, Harold, got a match?" and Harold shouting, "Yeah, my ass and your face!" before he laughs his way to the staircase.

I will ask Nina tomorrow night, when Mrs. Palazzetti is on duty, to check out the razor. If Mrs. P notices and asks me what happened to the blade, I'll say that I told Harold it was used up and he tossed it. They see each other only at shift change: relief and misery passing in the night.

I put the tweezers away but make a mental note to do my eyebrows soon, hoping that Dr. Hoffman will notice my renewed interest in personal hygiene and give me a regular appointment. I am still at the locker when Herlinda walks in, pausing to knock as she enters.

I take Daniel's shirt from its hook at the back of my locker. Since my wedding band was stolen, it is the only memento of him that I have. When I press it to my face there is the slightest scent of dry cleaning fluid lingering in the fabric. Herlinda takes it from me and holds it out.

"It is enough," she says. "He is there." She hands it back to me.

"Well?" she says.

I slip out of my robe and button myself into the shirt. It is black, with thin stripes crisscrossing it in orange and purple and blue. It hangs almost to my knees. I would never

have worn it while Daniel was alive; he was touchy about
his possessions.

"Remember what I told you, gringa," Herlinda says. I
nod. "Listen again. To rid your heart of a man, you must
take the shirt off his back and wear it day and night until
his smell is gone from it, until it has been covered over with
the perfume of your own soul."

"I'm not at all sure this is necessary."

"It will work," she says. "You wear it like I tell you, day
and night. When his smell is gone, you wash."

"You understand I'm only humoring you."

"It will work anyway," she says. "Come on. We are having a game in my room and you must join us."

"Herlinda," I say, "there are too many musts with you."

"Life is a must," she says. "We learned this game in the
detention center. In Miami. And it is a great one. Come."
She grabs my hand and pulls me after her. "Truth or Dare.
You will love it."

I let her tug me down the hall toward her room.

"Nothing good on the tube anyway," she says.

"Who's playing?" I ask as she pushes me into 306 and
closes the door behind us. The room is full, four women per
bed and the rest on the floor. Coffee is perched atop the sink
in the corner, resting her bare feet on the stainless steel rim
of the toilet.

"The usual suspects." Coffee scoffs. "All we need now is
Vanna White."

"Okay," Herlinda says. "The first person picks someone
and asks a question. You have to answer the question honestly or else take a dare from the one who asked. You can
ask anything, but remember, later someone will ask you."

"Hey," Coffee says, "I got a question. What's *she* doing in here?" She points at Three Sheets, who is standing at Herlinda's locker, fingering the beads of the rosary.

"I brought her," Nina says.

"You munching her rug now?" Coffee sneers. *"No mas Cubanas!"*

"Coffee" — Nina sighs — "I'll take just a thin slice of slack, no whipped cream. Got it?"

Coffee sideswipes Nina with her eyes, quick-juts her chin and smooths her face quickly back to cool brown stone before Nina can react. "What it is, girlfriend?" She takes a plastic pick from her back pocket and begins flicking it contemptuously through her hair. "You got another mo-fo headache or what?"

"Ladies," Herlinda says soothingly, "ladies, ladies, ladies. Please. Let's start before Harold misses us."

I crawl onto Herlinda's bed, easing into the thin space behind the backs of Lulu, Nina, Glenda and Emma. The cool of the plaster wall seeps through the fabric of Daniel's shirt.

"Cynthia's newest," Nina says. "Let her go first." She turns to me. "Pick someone."

"You," I say before thinking.

"What's your question, girlfriend?"

"What was your best scam?"

Nina props her hands behind her and leans her weight on her arms, letting her head roll back, eyeing the ceiling.

"It was glorious." She smiles. "I only netted around five grand, but it was glorious. The day after Reagan got shot, April of '81, I left for Mexico, hooked up with a DJ there who was so handsome I wanted to scream. He was a cross between Carlos Montoya and Elizabeth Taylor; he was stunning and had a great accent."

She stands and walks to a small space in the center of the tiny room, places one hand on her hip, raises the other in a gesture of recitation. She looks around slowly, vaguely dissatisfied with the size of her stage.

"We had mescal, lots of it, and sometime during the weekend we found — are you ready? Ten thousand full-color photos of Jesus, in two large wooden crates in an alley behind some bar.

"Guillermo said if I signed them, he would sell them. So there I went — Love, Jesus; Love, Jesus; Love, Jesus. God. I signed those suckers until I had blisters on my fingers. Monday night he cranked the wattage up until the signal from his station shot straight into the heart of Texas, though I doubt it made it up this far. Ten bucks apiece, real live genuine eight-by-ten full-color autographed glossies of the risen savior.

"I never thought they'd sell, but girlfriends, the good folks of the Lone Star State snapped them up like you wouldn't believe. The dollars flooded right into our little PO box in Juarez, and can I say it was a party? It was a party. I got so high I swallowed the worm."

Herlinda is trying with her brown eyes to burn a hole in Nina's satisfied smile, but Nina doesn't notice. She's still swooning over the memory of her handsome Mexican disc jockey. I can't help wondering which authority will first grab her for mail fraud.

"Right-on, Slick," Coffee says. "You be walking in red velvet slippers. You give the next question."

"I'll pass for now," Nina says, "but I reserve my turn for later."

"Here's one for *you*," Herlinda quavers to Coffee. She's still mad at Nina. "How many times have you loved a white man?" Coffee stands and looks for a deadly minute at Herlinda. Then she turns and spits viciously into the toilet before propping herself back on the sink.

"Well?" Herlinda snakes her arms beneath her breasts and hugs herself smugly.

Coffee closes her eyes, reaches behind her and presses the steel button. Air and water convulse in a high-tech federal flush, whooshing Coffee's reply to the sewage plant at the north end of the compound.

"My turn, I guess," Coffee says. "You got your answer." She turns to Lulu. "Why are you always so quiet?"

Lulu's terror at being questioned is so childlike that I am taken years back, reminded of home and my own fear at the battles my parents waged against each other. The first time I noticed the words "fuck you" scratched into the side of a Coke machine outside the recreation center where I practiced gymnastics every Thursday after school, I read them aloud. Mother grabbed my arm and shushed me harshly, looking around furtively while she told me never, ever, to say such a thing again. Later that night, when I lay in bed listening to her and my father arguing, as they did on those rare occasions when he happened through town, I understood in some vague way that the phrase was a powerful insult. I went to the top of the staircase and whispered down toward them, "Fuck you, fuck you, fuck you," until the music of my new and effective curse drowned the violence of the words they hurled at each other.

Lulu blushes and ducks her head. "That is the question?"

"Yeah," Coffee blurts. "That is my question. Why *are* you so damn quiet, girl? Truth or Dare."

"Truth," Lulu says. "Truth." She stares at her knees. "I think I am stupid. I think if I say things people will know how stupid." She folds her hands into her lap so gracefully that I see butterflies alighting.

Three Sheets stands next to the locker, crossing her eyes in an attempt to see the tears that have escaped silently onto her own Hummelesque pink cheeks.

"Your turn then," Herlinda says to Lulu. "Ask."

Lulu looks around the room until her eyes settle on Three Sheets. "Why are you crying?" she asks.

Three Sheets' fingers crawl across her cheeks like caterpillars, streaking her tears. "I have a toothache," she says.

Nina lets out one of her relentless sighs.

"Go tell Harold," she says to Three Sheets. "But if he gives you anything good for it, be sure you save some for me." She takes Three Sheets to the hallway and points her toward the dayroom. "Go on," she says gently, "just tell him what's wrong."

When Nina comes back into the room, she stands in front of me and says sternly, "Okay, Cyn. Enough of this bullshit. My turn now, and you can run, darlin', but you can't hide. Get out front here and talk to us. Get real. Why'd you kill your sister? Truth or Dare."

"I'll take the dare," I say. I can tell them the truth. I can answer that I did not kill my sister. I can lay that rumor to rest, but I need a different way out. Or maybe I only want their acceptance. Perhaps if I take some dare I will become one of them; I will no longer be the new girl, the one nobody is sure of.

"I dare you to tell the truth," Nina says.

Touché. And just what shall I say to this room full of thieves? That I did not kill my sister? That I don't even have a sister? Shall I tell them of Mummy and Daddy? Hubby? Or shall I say that I now suspect Daniel's actions jammed my ability to libidinally cathex? Shall I stutter or weep? Shall I say that it was, I swear to myself and whoever else will listen, clearly a matter of self-defense? Shall I say that as I near thirty-five and see the subtle changes in the structure of my face, I realize that it is the face of my father, and of his mother before him? That I wonder what legacy he left behind when he died, what pieces of his shredded life even now are hanging from my bones like war-torn flags, wrapping my skeleton in the death grip of a violently tortured man I never knew?

I look straight into Nina's eyes. "I'm afraid to look in the mirror," I say.

She props her chin on her fist and shakes her head sadly. "Fuck you, Miss Thing," she says. "The question is this: Why did you kill your sister? You a player or what?"

Three Sheets walks in with her index finger in her mouth, rubbing her gums.

"Oh, Mizz Cynthia," Coffee drawls sarcastically, "I jez *luh-uh-uh-huvs* a good old-fashioned solid kind of cop-out like that." She shakes her head slowly. "Jez loves it."

"All right then," I say. "Truth. I did not kill my sister. I don't even have a sister."

"Then why, girlfriend," Coffee says, "are you here?"

"You asked your question. I answered it."

"Very well," Coffee says, her lips hinting at a smile. "Glad you're awake. Your turn to ask."

"I'll pass."

"Nina's turn again then," Coffee says.

"And I," Nina says, looking around the room, "pick you, Mizzzz Cynthia. Tell us, my dear, if you didn't kill your sister, if you didn't sell drugs, if you didn't do anything criminal, then why are you here?"

They are all so very separate from me. But no different. We are locked in this place together. We have a common enemy. But we are all separate. I must join them or be marked as the outcast, the one who holds herself apart, who refuses to be one of them: the object of their antipathy.

"I am here," I say, "because I stabbed my husband."

Lulu takes a whisper of a breath, cups her hands over her mouth.

"Damn," Coffee says, "bitch cut her old man. Did you kill him? Or just wound the sucker?"

"I had to," I say. "He was killing me. Every single second of my life, he was killing me."

They sit, all of them, staring at me. I cannot understand why my eyes feel so dry, as though they've been baked in an oven.

I am lacing mailbags when Svejk taps me on the shoulder and says, "Dr. Hoffman wants to see you." I am momentarily elated, but then realize that I will run behind for the rest of the day, perhaps for the rest of the week, and it isn't yet lunchtime.

His office is somewhat more elegant than I had anticipated. I thought it would resemble the décor that prevails throughout Veritas. Though his desk is spacious and made of teak, I am certain that there is somewhere a numbered plate attached to it, however discreetly it is placed. It makes me feel as though I have some nebulous advantage in this, our first official encounter. Love serving thirty. I am ready to receive.

Wearing Daniel's now smelly shirt, sitting against leather, I stare at the good doctor in his good office, in all his polyester navy blueness, and worry that I will say the wrong thing, give him a statement that will enable him to keep me forever locked in Veritas.

Do I tell him I loved Daniel? That I hated him? That I loved him until the violence? That there were moments when I loved him even after? Should I attempt to cry? Should I claim PMS? Do I tell him that I would gladly have made myself Daniel's slattern, that I would have been, if I could, both wife and illicit lover to the man who was afraid of both, and am certain that, had I been able to attain such an intrinsic duality, I could have achieved the status of blood, the sticky liquid connector of body to soul? Do I catalogue the injuries? Get on my knees and beg his forgiveness?

Dr. Hoffman uncrosses his legs and asks, "Do you think you are God?"

That again. Back where we started. Is this man completely incompetent or merely obsessed?

"What I need, doctor," I reply, "is perhaps to develop more effective coping mechanisms. Or maybe I just need my lawyer." Although I understand that I need the doctor on my side, I feel incapable of extending even the most basic civility.

And I see that I have indeed offended him. He leans across his desk and looks at me for a long, menacing moment. His eyes look runny, like open wounds.

"The true optimist," he says at last, "when given a glass and asked if it is half full or half empty, simply picks up the glass and drinks what is in it."

Dr. Hoffman crosses leg over leg again and checks his watch before saying, "By the way, I'm assigning you a slot. I'll see you on Wednesdays at two o'clock. But where were we?"

"Playing God?"

"No. Wondering if you *think* you are omnipotent."

"No."

"Then how could you take a life? Who gave you permission?"

"I acted in self-defense. Correct me if I'm wrong, but I think that's recognized as a legitimate option. Legally, I mean. I think I'm within my rights to defend myself against someone who is attempting to kill me."

"I understood he was asleep when you killed him. How could that be self-defense? Wasn't he asleep?"

"Says who?"

"Forensics."

"Well, they weren't there, were they."

"They analyzed the evidence."

"Only two people were there. Daniel was there. I was there. There were no forensic specialists hiding in the bushes, were there? We could both be making better use of this time, don't you think, doctor?"

"I have no choice in the matter, Mrs. Mitchell. I have to present my findings to the court. I can't very well do that without arriving at an adequate evaluation of your circumstances and state of mind. Would you like to answer my question now?"

"I'm sorry, doctor," I reply, "I've forgotten what your question was."

"Why," he says flatly, "did you kill your husband? Did you think you were God? Do you think you are God?"

"Why do you keep asking me that? I've told you I do not think I am God. That's absurd."

"Why did you kill him?"

"I defended myself. That is all. That is all I did. It was not murder. It was self-defense." I focus on my breathing. I will remain calm.

"What gave you the right to make that decision? Why didn't you let the authorities handle it?"

I count slowly, silently, past ten to fifteen. Past fifteen to twenty. He folds his hands and waits for an answer. Past thirty. Almost to fifty before I can speak.

"The authorities," I say. "I called the authorities one time. They offered a restraining order. They said they would order him not to come within two hundred yards of me. They said they would give me a piece of paper."

When I return to the workroom from my appointment, shaking, I give my pass to Officer Svejk and take my seat in front of a fresh stack of mailbags. Tonight, I must find Nina. We'll smoke cigarettes and dream of cancer, dream of other cures.

I find myself tempted, as Svejk would put it, to "pull a Lulu." My sabotage, my intentional mis-threading, will prove to the Department of Justice that inmates cannot be trusted to do so much as a single afternoon's worth of honest labor. I will gladly do my part to help keep them all secure within the softly padded walls of their beliefs, their honest, hardworking convictions.

As I sit working the ropes, I wonder if they have ever awakened, in some three A.M. silence, to the sound of a solitary beating heart, and asked themselves where all the noise was coming from.

5 I remember being surprised when I flew down for the wedding. For our wedding. I had not been back to Texas since my father's funeral, more than eight years before. That call had come while I was at work, brainstorming with a couple of associates to come up with a promotion for some new cream or lotion that stopped itching on contact.

"He did it." The pain in her voice was magnified over the phone line.

"Did what?" I'd asked. Afraid to hear, but I'd asked any-way.

"Drank himself to death." A pause. "Well, not exactly." A longer pause. "He went over the divider on Central Ex-pressway."

"I'll fly down this evening," I'd said, not wanting to hear any more.

I'd stayed only long enough to do my daughterly duties, attend his funeral and make sure all the food was covered and put in the refrigerator before leaping onto a plane to escape back to New York. Alice, my sister, wanted to know why I couldn't stay a few days, spend some time with her and Mother. I'd blamed it on work.

The return flight had been almost empty. I curled in a window seat, wrapped myself in a blanket and wondered about the woman who'd sat near the back of the chapel and cried quietly during my father's funeral. None of us knew her; none of us had ever seen her. I wondered if there were others, and how many. I wondered if at some point I would begin to feel loss or sadness.

Eight years since then. From the air now, on the long, low, circling approach to DFW Airport, the land under the September afternoon sun looked overwhelmingly flat, as though it had been pressed solid and even beneath the weight of the huge blue sky. I had forgotten. The low foliage was baked to shades of pale green and light brown. After the deep greens and rolling hills of the northeast, it looked al-most hostile. But this time it was not death bringing me back. Daniel was bringing me back. We would have chil-dren. We would make a home. It thrilled and terrified me at once.

As I looked out the small, thick, scratched plastic window at the landscape below I had a moment of fear when I thought surely I was headed for disaster: I was not capable of raising a family; I didn't even know this man, Daniel, and I was being absolutely foolish to think I could be happy living so close to the place where I grew up. As a child and beyond I had dreamed only of escaping, and somehow I knew that Daniel and I would never be able to move beyond my own family tradition. The doubts built one upon the other until the fear was so overwhelming that it freed me from all apprehension. No matter what happened, it could not be worse than my imaginings. If the plane crashed, it would be nothing more than a reprieve from a future full of pain.

The mechanical whine and dull thud of landing gear moving into position brought me back to reality, and my fears suddenly seemed irrational. Even though Daniel and I hadn't known each other very long, only eight months, we knew that we loved each other. And thirteen years in Manhattan had given me more than a taste of the alternatives. I'd dated a series of well-spoken, intelligent, noncommittal and utterly self-absorbed men. The career? Flourishing, sucking out my soul so that it could grow according to schedule. Life was a rewrite. I'd had enough tedious meetings and lonely Manhattan nights — screaming fire engine sirens and take-out Chinese while I stared at the stacks of papers brought home from the office — to last three lifetimes. Daniel would change that. We would change that. We wanted children. We wanted to make a family.

The plane was going in circles. Waiting, as Daniel would say, for a parking place. He'd told me that I would be amazed at how much Dallas had changed, and even while I was still airborne, I could see what he meant. The city proper, downtown, had grown immense, and the buildings seemed made entirely of mirrored glass, all polished and new, clean and gleaming, glinting and sparkling in the afternoon sun. Spotless. Dallas struck me as trying just a little too hard, overcompensating for a vague but deep-seated sense of inadequacy. Nice enough on the surface, well-behaved and polite, but beneath that shining and well-scrubbed exterior was a city that took itself a bit too seriously yet not seriously enough. Maybe television had done that to it. Maybe it was J.R.'s fault. But Daniel's house, our home, was well north of Dallas.

My musings were interrupted by the deep drawling voice of the pilot over the intercom.

"Ladies and gentlemen, we apologize for the delay, but we're ready to land now, so make sure y'all're all buckled up. I'm pleased to inform you that my mother-in-law is aboard this afternoon, so I'm going to be trying for an exceptionally smooth landing. Thanks for flying American."

He landed the plane so smoothly, so gently, that I could not tell when we'd touched down.

When I came out of the ovenlike walkway into the refrigerated airport there were a few clots of smiling friends and relatives embracing, but no Daniel. A gate agent must have noticed my distress; he was kind enough to tell me that there'd been a last-minute arrival change. Through that gate right over there, I could take Surtran to gate 27E, where I might find my party.

After the subways of New York, the efficient electronic whoosh of the closing doors on the shining, driverless aluminum Surtran cars made me feel as though I were being hermetically sealed, like something perishable about to be shipped overseas.

He was waiting at the gate, hands stuffed in the pockets of his jeans as he looked this way and that until he spotted me coming down the corridor. When he first saw me, anger flashed across his face, he took a step forward, pulling his hands from his pockets, then stopped himself and smiled widely, leaned back against the wall. Opened his arms to receive me.

"I was scared you'd changed your mind," he said, wrapping me in a hug. He kissed me almost too gently. "I'm glad you're here."

"So am I," I answered. "But I don't have a clue where my luggage is."

"Welcome to DFW," he said. "Bigger than the island of Manhattan and, in its own way, almost as screwed up."

I felt myself getting scared as we walked toward baggage claim, and thought for a moment that I should flee back to New York, but I assured myself I was being silly and took Daniel's hand and told him about the landing.

"Oh, yeah." He smiled. "We call that painting the runway. Hard to do with a few hundred tons of metal coming in at a couple of hundred miles an hour. But what fun when it happens. Only a few of us can get it with any kind of regularity. For the rest, it's just luck. But ask anyone, that's one thing they'll tell you about me. I know how to land."

I teased him at first about owning a home in a giant amusement park, but soon I came to like living there. There was a long, tree-shaded drive entering off Interstate 45, posted with small, tastefully lettered signs: BEWARE OF LOW-FLYING AIRCRAFT; CAUTION, WATCH FOR CHILDREN, DOGS AND HORSES; SPEED LIMIT 10 MPH. The houses were on two or three acres apiece, nicely spaced, the settings private. Almost every home had a hangar in addition to a garage, and all were owned by pilots, either professionals or hobbyists. There was a clubhouse, with tennis and swimming, a nine-hole golf course and, down the road, a stable. The runway had a neon orange windsock.

That first night we spent in his house, I had a dream (can I legitimately call it that?) that I was on a conveyor belt, being processed by a series of loud machines: trimmed of fat, moisturized, powdered, painted, scented. I opened my eyes to a noise coming close, approaching from somewhere in the sky. Through the bedroom window I saw the approach of a small red, white and blue airplane as it swooped out of the sky and shot past, flying upside down about twenty feet or so above the blacktop runway that ran north to south down the middle of Rancho Milagro. I thought perhaps I wasn't fully awake but then felt Daniel's arm slip across my back. He raised his head and whispered, "Maniac," and then let his head fall back onto the pillow before pulling me close to him and wrapping me in the early morning warmth of his body. After a few more passes, the plane and its noise went elsewhere and left the sun hanging blissful and silent in the morning sky.

When I awoke for the second time, I found him leaning over me, holding a breakfast tray. There was fresh fruit salad, coffee with the faintest scent of cinnamon; there were huevos rancheros — handmade tortillas topped with fried eggs and shredded cheese and a delicious spicy red chili sauce — served with pinto beans and Mexican rice.

Later that afternoon, he took me flying. He called his plane a ragwing. It was a Piper Cub, red with a black bolt of lightning on either side and stitched fabric wings that would hold the plane in the air but crumple under the weight of a human.

On the ground, puttering down the runway, the plane felt flimsy and ill-made, and I doubted that we would ever get off the ground. But long before the end of the runway we lifted ever so gently into the air and began a long arcing turn that brought us around to a southbound path of flight. The engine didn't sound like much more than that of a large, deep-throated lawn mower, but its drone filled the cabin and made talking an effort. We curved around to the southwest and Daniel took us over Lake Dallas, its bottle-green surface broken in the hazy afternoon by an occasional leaping fish. A few diehards stood or sat on patches of sandy lakeshore with fishing poles in their hands.

I was enchanted, sitting there next to Daniel. I didn't know much about flying, but I could feel from the movements of the plane that he was an excellent pilot. We were fifteen hundred feet up, surrounded by blue, riding the occasional gust, but hardly buffeted, and I felt completely at ease, wonderfully safe in his care.

I could see from the calm on his face that he was entranced with flying, that it was dear to him. He was at home in the sky. Perhaps the mechanical aspect, the plane's performance, was part of it. But when I asked him, he said he liked the perspective, that looking down from such a height cast everyday objects into different focus, making them seem either beautiful or pathetic.

I looked carefully. The fishermen on the banks of the lake were beautiful that day, peaceful at the water's edge. The interstate, it seemed to me, was pathetic, cutting through the landscape like a razor, wounding it.

.   .   .

"Room service," Nina sings as she enters. "You ordered the Châteaubriand for two?" Emma looks up from her magazine and watches as Nina breezes into 304. I make room for her on the end of my bed.

"Help me practice my free association for Dr. H," she says. "Word Up."

"Cloud," I say, still not sure where I am, whether I have returned fully from flying with Daniel.

"Silver lining, of course."

"Plane."

"Ooh, vacation."

"Pilot."

"Mmm. What's that thing? Oh, yeah, the Mile High Club."

"Sky."

She squints an eye at me.

"Why all the flying stuff?"

"Just memories," I answer.

"Oh," she says caustically, "that explains everything." She grabs my wrist and looks at my watch. "Later," she says. "We're getting nowhere, and 'Jeopardy!' is about to happen." She's almost out the door when she turns and says, "By the way, there's a new girl."

She stands a moment longer, while Emma tosses her sad magazine toward her locker and takes up her make-believe oars. I feel strange as I follow Nina down the hall, blurry and ill-defined, as though my skin isn't functioning and the boundary between me and the space I'm walking through has collapsed. I watch myself walk down the hall and try to think like Herlinda, try to look forward to the happy ending, but the act of walking down this hallway may last indefinitely. We may never reach the dayroom. I maintain a constant distance between myself and Nina; that is the best I can do. I hope she knows where she is going.

Sometime later I find myself at one of the tables in the dayroom, racing through double solitaire with the New Girl. Nina and some of the others are at the television. While I don't remember getting here, I do remember following Nina into the dayroom, the relief of arrival, being introduced to a nameless face. But the memory feels borrowed, maybe stolen.

The New Girl stops playing suddenly and says, "You know what your problem is?" I take advantage of her pause to check through six or seven cards before looking up.

"You take things way too seriously," she says, slapping her final two, hearts, atop the slovenly stack of cards before her.

"You don't even know me," I say. But covertly I agree with her. There are times when I find my sobriety unsettling, even tedious. I don't talk about questioning myself. I don't tell her that sanity has been on my mind. Or that I think I'll be able to convince the doctor of my competence, though I am no longer certain of it myself. There are days lately when I feel a large word salad sitting green and lumpy in the base of my skull, waiting to be tossed. I know that if only I could surrender, embrace the dignity of the condition, the language of schizophrenia could be mine.

The New Girl has reshuffled her cards and is tapping them against the table with one hand and using the other to futz with her contact lens while she waits. I apologize and shuffle my cards.

"WHAT IS GROUNDHOG DAY?" Nina yells.

"Way too seriously," the New Girl says.

"I know it's only a game," I say. "Are we playing?"

"Yes." She starts to flip cards. "I'm playing. You may join in if you wish." She moves fast, matching black to red, seven on eight, six on seven. I cannot compete. I put my cards on the table and lean back to watch her. When she reaches to put an ace above her row, I see the scars.

"When did you try to kill yourself?" I ask. She plays on, unperturbed.

"Almost eight years ago," she says, slapping her cards rapidly against the table. "Almost eight years. At a time when I was serious about nothing, not even my desire to do myself in."

"So what *is* your name?" I doubt that she'll respond.

"WHAT WERE THE FIRST FROZEN FOODS?" Nina screams, her face mere inches from the screen.

"It's none of anyone's business, is it?"

"As matter of courtesy," I say.

"This is hardly the place for that sort of thing."

"How, then, did you end up here?"

"I got caught. You?"

"My lawyer said keep quiet."

"So why bring it up?" She pauses to look hard at me, holding the three of clubs above the rows of cards.

"Oh," she whispers, "wait a minute. You're the one who murdered her old man."

"WHAT IS ROY G. BIV?"

"I heard it was my sister."

"So did I," the New Girl says, "and I've been here less than twenty-four hours. I didn't buy it for a minute."

I don't know why I am talking to this woman. Or why I am sitting at this table playing a game about which I know next to nothing and care even less.

"WHO WAS HAMMURABI?" Nina bellows.

"Tell me you've never been a slave to love," the New Girl says.

"I've never been a slave to love. What's your name?"

"Why'd you murder your old man?"

"Says who?"

"You murdered your old man."

"I'm here for an evaluation, darling, not for murder. I haven't even gone to trial."

"WHAT IS NEW JERSEY?" Nina screams.

"New Jersey?" The New Girl looks up.

"The lowest suicide rate of any state in America," Nina calls to her.

"Excuse me," I say. "Either play cards or play 'Jeopardy!'"

The New Girl turns back to me.

"So why'd you kill him?" she says.

"He had greater heart-lung capacity and understood leveraged buyouts."

"Get real."

"Tell me your name."

"My name is Henry Kissinger. My legions of close friends call me Kissy. Why'd you kill him?"

"Kissy," I say, "give it a rest."

Three Sheets approaches.

"Final Jeopardy is next," she says. "Right after the brief commercial interlude."

"ALEX!" Nina shouts. "Alex. Baby. You hunk. You bruiser. You ex-Canadian sanitation engineer! Oh Alex, Alex, Alex! Beat me, fuck me, make me write bad checks!"

I stack my cards and place them in the center of the table.

"Kissy," I say, "let's play again real soon."

As I walk down the hall toward 304, I hear a sound coming out of it that I can't quite place. It is close to Emma's voice, but different, guttural, almost choking.

Nina is yelling at Three Sheets to leave the TV alone, and Mrs. Palazzetti snorts past me into the dayroom. There is something disjunctive lurking in the hallway.

When I get to my room, Emma is cross-legged on the bed, but she is not rowing. She's bent over at her nonexistent waist, her arms flopped in front of her on the bed, and she is crying. Sobbing.

I close the door behind me and turn out the light. Her sounds swell in the darkness, filling the room with pain; it is more than crying, more than sobbing, more even than weeping. It is agony.

I'm not sure what to do, whether I should call Dr. Hoffman. I say her name. Emma. What a beautiful name. I say it again, softly, trying to pull her away from the hideous place she has slipped into.

I hear her raise her head and wipe her face with her sheet; she sniffs and chokes and begins sobbing again. I walk over and sit on her bed, reach to touch her shoulder.

"No." She shudders. "No, don't."

I withdraw my hand. "Emma," I say.

She falls back onto the bed and pulls her blanket to her shoulders, snuffling and trying to catch her gasps.

"I want my baby," she whispers. Her words hit me like an electric shock. She sits up suddenly, as though pulled by strings. "They took my baby and I want my baby. I want my baby, I want my baby, I want my baby," she chants, whispering, cross-legged again and rocking, wrapped in her blanket. "My baby," she moans, "I want my baby. They took my baby. I want my baby."

I reach quickly, wrap my arms around her, hold tight before she can push away. I pick up her rhythm, the rocking.

"Shhh, Emma. There now. Shhh. You have to tell me."

"I . . ." She chokes. "They took my baby. I want my baby."

"Who?" I ask.

"They. That judge . . ." Her voice breaks again. Her sobs come from someplace deep inside her, so hidden that I cannot fathom it. I think for a long, awful moment that I can actually hear her heart breaking. I hold her and rock with her. "My baby," she whispers. "I want my baby."

"Dr. Hoffman — " I start, but she pulls away.

"He knows." She gasps, nose running, water pouring from her eyes. "He knows and he won't help me. I want my baby. Get away from me! Don't ever touch me! I. Want. My. Baby."

"What can I do?" I ask. "Do you want the doctor?"

"Don't touch me," she says. "Just don't touch me."

I cringe at Daniel's fist in the darkness, plunging toward my face. Daniel's boot, Daniel's hand, Daniel's mouth pulled cruelly open. Slapping. Back. Front. Back. Front. The stinging skin, the cracking bone. Daniel's need. Daniel's methodology.

"Get away from me," she says. "You stink. I don't need anything. Don't ever touch me."

I rise very slowly, swipe at the darkness to rid it of black memory, push down all feeling, all feeling, pushing, pushing. I go from the bed to my locker and concentrate on each small black button of Daniel's shirt. I fold its smelliness discreetly and put it carefully in the bottom of the locker. I dress myself for bed and lie down. *Don't touch me* floats in the room and I watch as it swirls toward the door and slips through the mesh like smoke, dissipating into the white-bright hallway. Don't touch me.

Emma sobs quietly now, of this world again, almost back

in control. I lie motionless, listening until I no longer can, until I feel as though my own ribs are squeezing my lungs empty, tightening within my chest to the point that there is nothing left inside but a heart-size knot of bone. I must not scream. I must not.

The hack comes jingling down the hallway, tapping on doors, yodeling that it's time to rise and shine, that a new and beautiful day has dawned on Veritas. The daylight is shocking. I can't quite reach the present; last night throbs in my head like a hangover. It's as though I'm bruised all over. Inside. Emma sleeps through the ordinary morning sounds of people waking and stirring, audible yawns, beds being made, teeth being brushed.

The voice in my groggy brain is confident; it belongs to a television announcer: *Contestants were chosen at random from our studio audience.* I stare out the window and forgive Emma. I let her sleep. She didn't know what she was saying.

Dr. H is wearing his stethoscope when he steps into the room. It is Friday, the day of the week when laundry is done and Dr. Hoffman performs rounds, a day to rinse the linens and evaluate mind-sets of the allegedly mad. Though no one has complained, I am convinced that the doctor wears his stethoscope in case he spies a particularly intriguing set of breasts and decides to take a closer look. I forgive him, too. Today I am full of forgiveness.

He stands next to Emma's form under the blanket and raises a thick eyebrow.

"She was upset last night," I say. "She wouldn't talk about it. I would have called you."

"Let's let her sleep," he says. "And how are you?"

"Well-adjusted."

He rewards me with a smirk.

"She had a baby? The courts took custody?"

The doctor looks at her and shakes his head slowly, robotically.

"No and yes," he says. "She had a baby, a little girl. She's a very disturbed young woman. I'm not at liberty to discuss it."

"But we're already discussing it. She told me she had a baby and that a judge took her baby. How do you expect me to help her if I don't know what's going on?"

"Cynthia," he says, "you are not here to help her. Let's do it this way. I'll be the doctor. You be the inmate. How does that sound?" He clucks his tongue sympathetically at Emma before leaving the room. I begin stripping my bed.

I am standing at my door holding my pillowcase stuffed with sheets when he comes out of 308, Nina's room, and in the moment before he notices me I see the way his horse-like face is melting. When he catches me looking he halts himself immediately, stopping the smile that would have spread from ear to ample ear if he had continued to daydream.

I'm surprised that I haven't noticed it before. I hope it's more than a crush. I hope they're in love. They would be good for each other: a well-traveled southern belle anarchist and a head-case shrink from Saint Louis. I'd like to see them together in the free world. My guess is that they could lead a couple of seriously unexamined lives, do a fine bit of American-style living before they exhausted themselves or Nina ran out of checkbooks.

.   .   .

Sunday morning, I'm waiting in the stairwell with the Catholics while the prison chaplain finishes an ecumenical service in the dayroom. Three Sheets and Kissy and several Black inmates are in attendance, listening raptly to the chaplain while he speaks poetic justice.

Just as they emerge, a priest makes his way upstairs, a dutiful and wide-eyed altar boy at his heels. The priest and the chaplain shake hands as they pass on the landing, and then the priest goes about setting up a makeshift altar on one of the cafeteria tables in the dayroom. The Cubans are mumbling to one another in Spanish, excited, it sounds, at the prospect of attending Mass. Herlinda tends them like a grandmother, smoothing a hair here, straightening a blouse there.

At the last minute, Coffee and Nina walk past where I sit propped against the back wall and take seats in the front row. The priest seems skittish, licking his finger and glancing up quickly as he turns each page of his missal. Though I crossed the line from lapsed to failed some years ago, his presence takes me directly to third-grade music class, where I almost discovered the sin of masturbation. Boys wore black trousers, white shirts, black ties. Girls wore light blue blouses under houndstooth jumpers that had slits where pockets ordinarily might be. This made it easy to reach in and tug down the blouse, keep it spiffy and neat, evidence of clean living. I was front row left in Room 103, giving voice to a hymn and wondering whether I wanted to be a nun, when I began to itch in the place one was never, under any circumstances other than bathing, supposed to touch. I shifted in my chair a few times, suffered as long as I could, until it went from itch to outright pain, and finally I snuck my right hand through the false pocket. I was trying to be discreet, not to let the movement of my hand show, and maybe that's why I discovered that my fingers, after stopping the itch, were lingering. The feeling they gave was comforting, secure and exciting at once, but I still understood that it was one of those things the nuns called Unspeakable.

When Sister Helena slammed her spidery digits against the piano, glaring at me as only a nun can, I felt heat rushing into my cheeks and froze. She gave me her best and most damning evil eye, as though my action had been directed at her and the insult were intentional.

"Where is your hand? Show me your hand!" I did so with innocence quickly recaptured, slipping my hand from beneath my skirt and holding both hands before me, trying desperately not to cry. I did not look at my classmates, but I knew they were staring at me to see how I'd hold up under the glare of Sister Helena's small eyes. Embarrassment flushed pink on my cheeks, and then became for pity's sake the rosy glow on the face of an angel. I spent an eternity, at least the rest of that week, convinced that I would one day face the gates of hell, for I hadn't the first idea of what words could possibly explain such behavior when I entered the confessional.

I look up in time to see the priest hesitating before giving Coffee and Nina the transubstantiated wafers, and remember asking my mother, before my First Holy Communion, "But what does it *taste* like?" I wondered even then if I would ever gain sufficient faith. Dr. Hoffman has told Nina that the Jews have a lock on guilt, but in the shame department, I'm sure, in the Department of Intrinsic Shame, Catholics are untouchable. I wonder if the doctor would admit that it's possible I craved Daniel's malfeasance for its redemptive possibilities.

I bow my head, ducking stray blessings as the priest finally utters, "Go in peace."

As I watch him raise his holy hand to send forth the final benediction, I'm convinced that had I been able, when I was in public relations, to conceive of a marketing plan as brilliant as that of Original Sin, I might well have enabled some lucky corporation to succeed in taking over the world.

6   Dr. Hoffman has chosen a partly cloudy day with tem-
     peratures in the low to mid eighties to administer
     the first battery of tests. The weather is fine.
I am here in my room, *sans* Emma, looking out the window and realizing that I spend too much time looking out
the window. The weather is fine. The Texas sky is beautiful,
even though my view is sliced into ribbons by razor wire.
But I can look past that. I can see it or not see it.
Waiting here for one of the hacks to come and tell me

that the doctor will see me now makes me feel unsettled. I should be downstairs in the workroom, lacing mailbags. Not that I look forward to that, but I've learned to rely on the routine to ease me through the days. If I concentrate on it, on just doing the work, I can escape the constraints of hours, minutes and seconds. Time flies when you ignore it. It is when I am thinking about Daniel, about how it ended, that time slows to a crawl. That's when I count every second as a precious addition to the distance between then and now.

I don't like to think that I married him out of desperation. But it occurs to me sometimes, when I'm looking for explanations, when I say to myself, "How on earth could you have . . ." Perhaps one of Dr. Hoffman's tests will have a section like that, where I will be required to finish open-ended sentences.

I wonder what I would think if I met Daniel today, how I would see him. I wonder if he succeeded, finally, in shattering the image-bending lens of loneliness through which I viewed the world at that time in my life. I saw him then as fine-featured, athletically built, with an edgy kind of intelligence in his blue eyes and an adventurous spirit. Well-traveled and worldly. Kind-hearted, but strong enough to survive a difficult situation. I saw him as full of love for me, overflowing with love for me, and thirsty for the love I had for him.

I thought, the first time I was before him, that he was inspecting me. He undressed me slowly, to the sound of rain against the windows, a tiny moan escaping from his throat when I at last stood naked before him. He knelt and kissed my belly, ran his hands over my hips and legs and ankles, touched a finger to my toes. He stood and took my face in his hands, kissed me gently, stepped back. He stood silently for a long moment.

"You're beautiful," he whispered.

The curve of his shoulder astonished me.

The door bangs open, pulling me from reverie, and the hack motions to follow. I don't know where I've been.

The window unit in Dr. Hoffman's office emits a low whistle when the compressor comes on. It sounds almost like the first four notes of "Hail to the Chief" repeated, repeating. It could inspire military behavior. It could aggravate an existing condition. I mustn't be distracted. I must concentrate, do my best.

"What do you see?" he says, holding up the first card. I look carefully; I peer at it.

I see blood.

"Chrysanthemums," I say.

"How about this one?"

Blood again.

I tell him something. I name an object.

"And this?"

Blood. But my voice responds, says something else.

He stops to make a note and then holds up another.

"Azaleas."

"What do you see here?"

They all look the same.

"And here?"

"A tree. An oak, I think."

"This one?"

"I'm afraid it's more flowers."

"That's perfectly fine," he says. "Just tell me what you see."

"You're looking for spontaneous reactions?"

"I want you to tell me what you see."

I would like to be specific and realistic, but I can hardly tell him that what I see are black blots of blood on cream-colored pieces of cardboard.

"This one?"

Blood. I have to see something else. Make something up.

"And this?"

"Shiitake mushrooms," I say. "No, wait. No. That's not it, that's not what I see. Give me a second." He's staring at me. "Yes," I stammer, "shiitake mushrooms, that's it. Shiitake mushrooms."

"Calm down," he says. "Just calm down. Take a moment." He holds the card before me. There was so much blood. And now I see ink.

I try to laugh. What's wrong with me? I look toward the floor and notice my hands and look back at the card and then again, a quick cautious glance at my hands. I did not see what I just saw. I did not.

They've gone dead; my hands have gone dead. Two useless appendages of gray-blue flesh in my lap, as if tossed there. I can't move them. Calm down, the doctor says. I want to get away from them. Very very fast. This is important. They are no longer part of me. I don't understand. They have died but won't fall off and won't move and won't go away. They are here in my lap, I tell you, dead things in my lap, and there is nothing I can do, they are *dead*. And yes, goddammit, the whole mess *does* look waxy. That's it exactly, as if they're made of wax. I know what I'm talking about, doctor, I've seen it up close, you know, dead flesh, *the skin of the dead*, and these things in my lap are very much just that. Very much. I can't bear this. There was so much blood.

"Shiitake mushrooms," I say. "Definitely shiitake mushrooms." My voice is alive. I pay attention as he holds up the cards. I respond and don't look at my hands. Don't look. Don't dare. He makes notes, holds up cards. I answer, he makes notes. Blood. Flowers. Blood. Trees. Blood. Ink. Trees and flowers. Stay with the safe things, flowers and trees. The last things Daniel saw.

He lets the last card fall face down on his desk and scribbles out a paragraph. His penmanship is minuscule, and although my eyesight is excellent I can't make out what conclusions he's drawn and my hands are down there somewhere.

He leans back in his chair and crosses his legs and smooths his tie. Why is he pointing his tie at me? Can't he see? Doesn't he notice? *My hands are dead.*

I'm sure he thinks the thing he's making with his mouth is a smile, but I know very well when teeth are being bared. "Are you all right?" he asks.

I shrug at him and do not scream, "I SAW A LOT OF BLOOD, DR. HOFFMAN, AND MY HANDS HAVE JUST DIED, DR. HOFFMAN, MY ARMS FROM THE ELBOWS DOWN! Help me, Dr. Hoffman, there was so much blood I'm scared enough to trust you. It came out red and more. *It came out red and red and red and red.*"

I look at him, shrug at him, I don't say, "There was a knife." He stares at me and plays with his tie, aims it again, right at me. I look away and realize that he must know all about it. How thick and sticky it is, and how it dries black as ink.

"Why don't you take this one back to your room," he says. He holds a folder out to me. "You'll be given ninety minutes to finish. It's true-false."

"Dr. Hoffman," I say, "I'm feeling ill. May I take it to-morrow?"

"Is something wrong with you?" he asks. "Are you coming down with something?"

"I think so," I say. "I think I should go and rest."

"Go then," he says. "I'll notify Svejk."

He doesn't see what a struggle it is for me to get the dead things out of the chair and out the door and down the eternal hallway. It is high tide in the stairwell. I am drenched when I emerge and I don't know how long I was in there.

I edge along the wall so that I won't spoil the shine Three Sheets is trying to put on the floor in front of her room. She is chirping and doesn't look up to see me dragging my hands toward my room. She crawls slowly across the tile and adds yet another rent wad of tissue to the mess she's making as she cleans.

I open my door and pull my hands in after me before closing it and sliding to the floor. Everything is too bright; the grays and greens shriek at my closing eyes. Three Sheets' chirps pop through the window one by one, white and shining like Ping-Pong balls, falling to the tile and bouncing around the room. I duck this way and that, this way and that as they ricochet off the walls. I force myself to look at what used to be my hands, wonder if the death in them will spread up my arms and into what's left of the rest of me. I wonder why I am dying, why my body has chosen this moment to give itself up.

Daniel is doing this. The memory of him is doing this.

Louisa brings the water, puts it in front of Herlinda, walks over and stands quietly at the door to the workroom. Maroon canvas mailbags are everywhere, surrounding us. Herlinda moves a trolleyful of them between the door and the table where we sit, sits down across from me and places the mayonnaise jar full of water where it will catch morning sun from the window.

I am not officially here. Officially I am in my room, too ill to lace mailbags, too ill to take Dr. Hoffman's true-false quiz. Thursday. He has sessions with Nina, then Glenda, then Three Sheets, back to back. He will be busy from ten until one-forty, and then too tired to shuffle about looking for trouble. Harold is upstairs in the dayroom, trying to keep himself awake by watching the late morning game shows, having been roped into a double shift when Mrs. Palazzetti called to say she would be staying home with her sick children today. I hope she is playing hooky. I hope she's gone to the mall or to lunch with a friend, or maybe just stayed in bed with six or seven magazines and a few pounds of chocolate. I hope her husband treats her well, but I don't hope too much. In truth, I imagine him to be a beer-slugging, swaggering brute whose work involves petroleum products and who usually comes home not quite drunk, sobers a bit over dinner, sits down after in his lounger to spend the evening belching in front of the television, swilling Budweiser until the news hypnotizes him into something resembling sleep. I'm sure Mrs. Palazzetti has adapted to his postindustrial malaise. She keeps the children quiet.

Herlinda turns the jar slightly to the left, moves it a centimeter or so toward me, her dark brown eyes focused on something she sees inside it. She moves the jar again and the water prisms the sunlight, splintering it into rays of red, green and yellow, indigo, orange and blue. A violet shadow falls across the table and onto my crossed arms, my still numb but somehow folded hands.

"Your grandmother stuttered," Herlinda says. "You worry about that. Sometimes you are afraid you also might stutter. When you're nervous."

I am about to smile at her when I realize that she's right. What she has said she could not possibly have known.

She sits waiting for confirmation. I give a small nod, something I can manage.

"You blame yourself," she says quietly.

"For what?"

"You tell me."

"For my grandmother's stuttering?"

"Such silliness. It doesn't become you."

"For what, then? What are you looking for?"

"It's what you are looking for, gringita. I only help. Believe. What I see or don't see in the water. I can help. But you must participate."

"Herlinda. Now is not a good time."

"Why do you stare so at your hands?"

"You tell me."

"You blame yourself, that's why. As you always have. You blame only yourself."

"That's not true."

She leans close to the jar, looks at it, through it, beyond it. The colors of sunlight streak her caramel skin. She looks until her eyes begin to water, welling deep with tears from the brilliance of the light.

"I tried to warn him," I say.

"I'm sure," she replies, dabbing at her eyes with a shirt sleeve. "You should have warned yourself. What did you tell him?"

I don't remember. Perhaps I was in such terror of him that I could not admit it even to myself, much less to him. The first time it happened, I do remember, was a Sunday, late afternoon, and I was in my chair in the living room, reading a novel. Daniel was on the couch, reading, getting up every few minutes to poke at the fire. He was in his blue corduroys and a gray cotton sweater, and his restlessness was contagious. I mumbled something about the fire not needing so much attention, not even looking up from my book until I heard the clatter of the poker against the brick mantel.

Before the noise had stopped, before I saw him move, his hand struck my chin, knocked my eyes closed. A white gash of pain and light cut through my brain. I felt teeth crack, explosion, eyes tight closed as I fell back, back, heard his bellow, the sickening thuds of his fists against brick as he bloodied his knuckles on the mantel. I stayed as I was; I did not move. I stayed on the floor by the chair, opened my eyes. I would not move. I closed my eyes. I heard someone trying to scream.

I don't know how long. When I heard him back at the fire, retrieving the poker, I opened my eyes to see him sweating or crying or both, on all fours, almost panting.

And then he was kneeling next to me, mumbling I'm sorrys, while numbness spread through me as slowly and quietly as water turning to ice.

I thought to speak but my jaw would not move. Eventually he left me there and went to bed. I stayed where I was that night, all night. I did not sleep. I did not stir. I listened at dusk to the giddy screams of teenagers careening down Church Road in convertibles, listened all evening to the lessening hum of weekend traffic on the distant expressway, and later, in the small hours of morning, to the garbage truck that circled through Rancho Milagro collecting neat green bags of refuse, its brakes howling in the night like a wounded dog.

I didn't know what it was exactly, but knew it was something more than Daniel's unprovoked violence that was filling me with such fear.

"Cynthia?" Herlinda taps gently. "Cyn?"

The sunlight throws colors across her arm. A breath of air feels good. A slow deep quiet breath of air.

"Tell me."

"I can't."

"You can."

At a certain point, after it had gone on a long time, it became like listening to an old favorite record. You know where all the skips are, so you prepare for them, mentally. You prepare for them, and if you listen to the song often enough, over a long enough period of time, then you automatically anticipate the skips, the nicks. And you start to like them almost, just because they've become so familiar. So certain. So known. You keep playing the record because you love the song, and the skips that you used to hear as an interruption of the music have become part of the music.

"Cynthia. Talk to me."

I do not wish to answer.

"I'm here, Cynthia. Tell me."

"Why?" I ask. "So you can tell your girls? What is it they whisper? Tell me what it means, '*Quien mató a su hermana?*' What does that mean, Herlinda? What are they whispering about me? It is me, right? I'm the one they're always talking about?"

"Please. They are foolish, they don't mean anything. It is their way."

"What way?"

"They ask who killed your sister. I will tell them to stop. Please don't be angry at them."

Why am I talking to this woman? I don't know her. She

doesn't know me. Am I actually sitting here listening to a Gypsy tell me what the future holds? I cannot bear it. Daniel told me what my future would hold. He told me it would hold our love for each other and the children we would have and how we would grow closer and closer as the years went by. He told me how he would cherish me, cherish our family. Come to Texas, he told me. Come and be my wife. He told me. The future. It is too much. I am surrounded. They are all, everyone in the unit, pressing in close, pushing constantly at me, breathing their trashed lives down my tired and beaten neck, mingling their sad pasts with my own, becoming part of the inadequate present. Why won't they leave me? I understand that I will carry them as I do him. I will carry all of them with me for as long as I live. I will never escape any of this.

"Where are you going, Cyn?"

I am at the door when I realize Herlinda is addressing me.

"To my room," I say. Did I stutter? Carefully this time. "I am going to my room, Herlinda. Thank you. I think I will try the water another time."

"Rest," she says after me, whispering. Her word slips past me, near the floor, and floats down the long hallway toward the staircase. I am too weary to chase after it, to try to catch it.

I do not know where she has come from, but she is here now, dressed in red, dressed in a red dress, dressed for dinner. I wonder where she is going and where she has come from. I wonder what her real name is, but mostly I'm thankful that she's so busy talking, she hasn't noticed my hands.

"*Aaaand,*" she is saying, "for some reason I was able to

recognize the symptom even while it was happening to me. I had just escaped from the massive entrails of Tower Records on lower Broadway, you know the one, and pushed through the revolving doors into a cold and snowy February, late morning, wind about to blow the bus over, and was walking, I hoped, toward the offices of my most recent shrink, a cute blond guy I liked to call Dr. Hank, who didn't know me from Adam's housecat. Listen to me, Cynthia, this is important. People were rushing along, the way they do, you know, and the sidewalks were as slippery as Liberace, but everyone was hurrying to wherever, you know — appointments, meetings, brunches — and inside my head, honey, all I could hear was this voice going, 'Hot-Cold–Hot-Cold–Hot-Cold–Hot-Cold,' over and over and over. Let me tell you, sweetheart, it scared the shit outta me. I prayed. Do you hear me? I *prayed* to God to please make another thought intrude? No no Nanette. Nothing. Nada. Just Hot-Cold–Hot-Cold–Hot-Cold."

She lets her head fall forward until her long brunette hair is hanging over her face, just touching her knees, as she sits propped on Emma's bed. Evidently there is not much that Kissy is afraid of.

"Even while it was happening," she says, "I knew it was dangerous. I had just bought a tape of Barber's 'Adagio for Strings' — do you know that piece; it's incredible — so I was hanging on to that and just watching my feet fall one in front of the other and it was that mushy kind of ice coming down that's not snow and not sleet and not really anything, it doesn't even have a color, but you can slip in it and bust your butt, until I was inside Dr. Hank's building going up in this ancient frightening I mean really creaky elevator which carried me and a woman with a schnauzer who had muddy paws, the schnauzer that is, to the third floor. I went right on in, Hot-Cold–Hot-Cold–Hot-Cold, on in to the waiting room just as I did every Tuesday and every motherfucking Thursday. There was one chair and a bookshelf and a radio that played what should have been soothing music but instead it was Wagner. I'd rather listen to Tammy Wynette than Wagner.

"That's when it occurred to me, Cynthia, through all the goddam *relentless* noise going on in my head, I mean I didn't even recognize the voice shouting the Hot-Colds at me, it occurred to me that it *might* be time to go back on the medication.

"So while I was waiting to see the doctor I stood up and removed my coat and hung it in the closet and put my cassette into the pocket and closed the closet door and turned to look out the window and saw all those hundreds of people down there, all rushing to their appointments. And then the weirdest thing happened. All of a sudden these thought balloons popped out of their heads. I saw all of them at once and they were walking through the ice storm, and every last godforsaken one of them was thinking — I could *see* this, you know, see their thought balloons — every last one of them was thinking the same thing: *What the fuck am I doing here?*

"And once I became aware of this? Once I really looked at them and saw in their faces and their postures and even their walks all of the turmoil and worry they were carrying around? Honey, I suddenly saw that I, Missy Kissy, was relatively well adjusted." She tosses her head back, flipping her hair dramatically.

"So instead of asking for a truckload of Prozac," she says, "I walked into the office and stretched out on the couch and said, 'Hank? You're fired.' And I got up and got my coat and my adagio and took myself to the movies."

I'm looking at her, and looking, perhaps even staring. I don't know how long she's been talking. I know I heard her, but I can't make sense of a single word she's said.

I think she notices this, for she sits quietly, staring at me with her lips twisted into a smirk.

"Darling Cynthia," she says now, "I can see you're having one of those abominable days. You look like death warmed over. Let me explain. I just want to assure you that it's not as bad as you think. The thing is, I want you to know that you're okay. Okay? I mean, look at me. My family, darling, the members of my esteemed family are thieves, each trying to shoplift emotional sustenance from the empty shelves of another's soul. And my father, dear Cynthia, my father was merely the blunt instrument with which my mother chose to beat herself over the head. Get what I'm saying? See?

"All that, but here I am, still kicking. And the point of my sermon, honey bunch, is that you should *never, never, ever* lose your sense of humor."

The point of her sermon?

"Kissy," I say. "Whoever you are. I have to take a test. The doctor has given me this MMPI thing to take and I have to be alone now so I can take this test he has given me. Dr. Hoffman has given it to me. I have to take it."

She doesn't seem to understand. She is staring at me as though she is sane and I am mad, although I know full well the opposite is the case. The walls are melting. What is happening? Kissy, too, is baring her teeth at me. Why are they all so hostile? Why is everyone growling? I hope to maintain my composure. I need to be in a corner, in a corner of the room. I brush past Kissy's bared teeth. That's where I would go when Daniel got his look. It was easier to take with my back pressed into the corner. I could leave my body there and step aside while he finished his business. Why is Kissy looking at me that way? Not at all like Daniel. She looks frightened. She is moving for the door.

"Where are you going?" I ask.

"Cynthia," she says, "you just stay right there. Right where you are. I'll be back in a few minutes and we'll talk."

I crouch in the safety of the corner. He couldn't hit me from behind that way. Sometimes I got so far away from myself that it didn't even hurt while he was kicking.

7

When I wake, everything is white. White everywhere, unbroken. The walls, the floor, the ceiling, the light. Unbroken, brilliant white. It burns my eyes.

The sheets, the blanket, the cold metal bedframe. White. The sound in this room, the silence is white. My breath, the coming and going of white air. Molecules dancing are white. Past and future are white. Present, too tenuous to see. White everywhere. My arms glare pink and green, shooting out of the huge sleeves of this very white hospital gown. My feet are hidden in white socks. How long have I been here? I make no noise.

I sit up. I lie down. I tug at sheets, ineffectually, see the pink and green arcs my arms leave hanging in the air. Molecules dance. Atoms dance. I disintegrate, disappear into the dead or alive atmosphere of this room, this cell, this place of no escape. All time is now. All is survival.

Where is the noise? The sound? Birds chirping? TV blaring? The chattery Spanish of the Cubans? Where is all the noise that ebbs and flows through the halls, rising and falling like the tides, sometimes becoming a storm? I am surrounded by nothingness. It is maddening.

How far back? How far can I go in the white and silence of now? How far back? I wait yet again for sleep.

The floatingness of it. Swoosh-swoosh rhythm. Poom-poom, poom-poom, poom-poom. Liquid. Summer pond. The terror and ease of it. The muffled touch of Other. There is only now, momentary awareness. Momentary being, and then the darkness again until a slow growing something swells awake in liquid, surrounded, floating, breathes in liquid, sucks and blinks, startles at new noise, turns an eye toward skin-filtered light. Movement, touch of one, poom-poom, poom-poom, not yet arrived, not yet lost of the place before.

That memory is light. Brilliant with whiteness, alive with light. There was the tunnel leading from the place of light. There is this between time, this liquid place, time present in this place without time, past not yet lost, future yet ungained, this time soft and momentless. The touch of Other. No other. My other . . .

The beat of the large heart, the flutter of the small. The deafening roar of Mother.

I knew her fears. Her joys. I knew her touch, not as something separate, but as part of me. I knew her past; the physicality of it was me growing inside her. The memory of it was hers and all who came before her, and before, and before. All the way back, the memory was hers and so the memory became mine. I knew. And I knew the journey through the tunnel, toward the new light, would bring amnesia.

The other touch, this one also I knew. The heavier one, the stronger one, the touch that came with deep noise and pressed her belly so rarely. The pressure of it. Big heart beating bigger. I knew her fear when the heavy touch came. I knew the heavy touch. The history of it. The beginning of it, the crawling. I knew her fear even then.

I start at the sound of my mother screaming, awake to the noise of her trying to scream, the weak noise of her effort echoes in my skull. I was eight by then. That is how I mark my ninth year. It is the year my mother first tried to scream.

She was not successful. It came out broken, inadequate, afraid to take itself for what it was, afraid of its own terrifying reality. It came out aimed at my father's upraised fist, and pitched above the range of the human ear.

I hid in the closet.

I don't know how long I've been here. This silent place. This white place. I remember Kissy coming back that day but she did not come alone. She brought the doctor, and he must have brought me here, to white and silence. At first it was a relief.

For a while, for some however many days, I counted the times they brought food. Divide by three and that equals a day. The food comes through a slot in the door. But I've lost track. The food, though. The food has no taste, but at least the food has color. Pink ham. I didn't eat, because inside the pink, on the slimy surface of the pink, there were the colors of fish scales — turquoise and green on the pink ham, blue and silver on the pink ham. Like the skin of my arms sticking out of the holes in this white gown. My skin is blue. My skin is green. Mrs. Palazzetti did not appreciate it when I accused her of trying to poison me. I realized immediately my mistake and let her stand there while I wolfed down the peas, just to prove my point. I ate the green things, I ate the yellow bread, gummy though it was. I ate the off-white sauerkraut, too, though I told her that culinarily, it was disgusting to serve fish with sauerkraut.

"It's not fish," she said. "It's ham."

"Mrs. P," I said, "I'd like a vegetarian diet. From now on, I'd like a vegetarian diet, please."

The light in the center of the ceiling stays on constantly. My eyes burned for some time. Again, I don't know how long. After the burning, it became a tickling on the back of my eyeballs. I knew I couldn't really be feeling that, but I did. Now, however, my eyes are used to it. I am adjusting to my environment. I can sleep while staring straight at the light, although it is an ugly bare bulb inside a wire cage. Even the light bulb is in jail. I wonder if this ability I've developed, to sleep while staring at light, is normal. I wonder if anything is or has ever been normal. I wonder if it makes Dr. Hoffman angry that I am doing so well in this room. I miss Nina and Emma and Kissy.

I miss my friends?

No books. No magazines. No one to talk to. No one to hear. Sit and look at the light. Look at the walls of spotless white. Look at the white floor, the white gown, the white sheets. The white blanket. My skin is blue today. Is it today or tonight? Good morning, Cynthia, how are you? Me? Just fine, thank you. Yes, yes, a bit, I have to sit here and think all day. Or perhaps sleep all day and think all night. I'm afraid I don't know which is which. No, not the sleeping or thinking; those I can differentiate. It's day versus night that's giving me trouble. Where'd you say the doctor went? Did he say when he'd be back?

It's so quiet in this place I can hear my own pulse somewhere deep inside my ears. Whoosh-whoosh, whoosh-whoosh. Is that what my life sounds like?

The floor is spongy beneath my feet as I wobble toward the door. There's the hack now, coming down the hall, mouth blatantly open, braying numbers, but there is no noise. I think perhaps I've gone deaf, but the thought is hardly alarming. There is no sound. No jangle of keys. No squish-soft footfalls. No polyester swishing of thighs. I stand in the door and see Janna across the hall. When did they move her here? She is hanging by her neck, her oddly small neck, which she has managed to fit into the miniature hangman's noose on the cord of her venetian blinds. She's smiling at me, a smile of mischief, the smile of a practical joker. She wiggles her toes and smiles even more broadly.

"I can die and never feel pain," she whisper-shouts across the hall. She cups a hand over her mouth: Speak no evil.

The floor is still spongy, spongier than ever. My socks are wet. I remove them and try to find a place to hide them, but the hallway is spotless. I drape them over the doorknob of the unoccupied room next to mine. That is just how my lungs feel, like wet socks hanging inside my ribcage. I wish I could breathe. Where is Emma? Where is Dr. Hoffman?

I peek through the window of a room down the hall.

Someone is sitting on the bed, weeping. It is a man with broad shoulders and neatly combed brown hair. He raises his head slowly, convulsing with deep, racking sobs, hopeless, pathetic, oh-so-silent sobs.

It is my father.

He is alone.

He knew this would happen.

He sees me looking and smiles weakly, from very far away. He shrugs. Waves me on.

I turn from the window and see Nina and Dr. Hoffman waltzing down the hall, keeping perfect time to a music I cannot hear. She's in her blue bathrobe, he's in tie-dyed surgical scrubs, grinning like an imp.

In the dayroom, Coffee is watching "Wheel of Poets" on television. There are Pat Sajak and Vanna White, looking for a word or phrase that rhymes with *antinomian.* Coffee sits on the couch, her feet on the coffee table, drawing strength from her hatred of Pat and Vanna. It makes perfect sense.

I run slowly back toward my room. The floor is made of rubber and I am bouncing down the hall, bouncing high off the floor, tumbling in slow motion down the hall to my room in Veritas, or to my home in Rancho Milagro, or to my bedroom in the house of my parents. Janna swings from her noose, smiling.

"You'll have to stand in line when you get there," she says, "but even the devil takes American Express."

I know I want to wake up, I know this is a dream, but I do not know where or when it began, and I cannot begin to fathom what kind of nightmare I will wake up to.

He's wearing a new suit. Or perhaps it's an old suit, pinstripe and infrequently worn. His stomach bulges slightly over the waistband as he stands behind his desk. Has he put on weight? He's shorter than I remembered and has on a yellow paisley necktie. Hoffman has dyed his hair red and is combing it straight back these days.

I am wearing men's boxer shorts, that blue color, and a white Fruit of the Loom V-neck T-shirt. Little green shoes with soft rubber soles. The better to keep you from running, my dear. Mrs. Palazzetti called them Peter Pans when she handed them to me in that room and told me to put them on. After all the white, the colors were dazzling.

"How was your shower?" the doctor asks.

"Wet," I reply. "But for the first time in I don't know how long I am clean. From head to toe."

"Very good," he says. "Have a seat. For the first time in weeks, you have had a shower. Have a seat."

"Why am I wearing these things?" I ask.

"Procedure," he says. "Standard operating procedure, don't you know?"

Without recognizing it, he's picked up her phatic communication, Nina's conversational *don't you know*. As if we could also become, don't you know, ever the best of friends.

"Dr. Hoffman," I say, "would you be so kind as to turn the air conditioning down a little? It's cold in here if a girl's in her skivvies."

He reaches behind and hits a switch; the whistling fades and he turns to prop his chin on one palm. With his other hand he picks up a folder. Mine, I presume, though I've never had the pleasure. I wonder if I should permit the fly of these shorts to fold open when I sit down. I wonder if he'd get flustered if I sat here with the fly open, acting as though everything, including him and me, was normal.

I sit decently. I fold my hands in my lap. I control them.

For the most part they are alive. They turn gray only once in awhile. The other times, I've learned to ignore.

"What I'd like to know," Dr. Hoffman says, "is if you think you could do the rest of your time where we have you now."

"Here in your office? Won't I be in the way?"

"You know what I mean, Cynthia. Are you comfortable on Two?"

So I am on Two. The infamous Two. Two is white. But I didn't see Janna, or I saw her only in the dream. I didn't see leather restraints. What is it about Veritas that compels all of these women to lie?

"Dr. Hoffman," I say pleasantly, "I'm just trying to cooperate and get this thing behind me as quickly and painlessly as possible. Put me wherever you wish."

His pained expression, as though he just realized his sinus headache is *not* going to go away on its own, tells me I've given the wrong answer.

8 At times I feel like breaking things.

True. *True.*

I put off until tomorrow what I should be doing to-day.

Very true. *True.*

My table manners are not as good in private as when I am dining out.

Sometimes true. *False.*

I am an agent of God.

Aren't we all? *False.*

I have frequently wished I were a girl. (Or, if you are a girl) I have never regretted being a girl.

This is only a test.

True, true, false, true.

Tell me, doctor, what does the MMPI tell you? The Minnesota Multiphasic Personality Inventory, *ooh-la-la*. Give me some results. Categorize me. Peel the adhesive off that label and apply it neatly. Smooth out the bubbles.

I'd like to add one little Kissyesque question to the how-ever-many-hundreds there are in this test booklet: What the fuck are we doing here?

Have I ever been sorry that I am a girl?

Well, doctor, *I enjoy being a girl.* Maybe not when Daniel was showing me a thing or two and I wanted him to have to take it like a man. But don't let me give you the wrong impression. Most of the time I just wanted him to stop. Is that question here? I wanted him to stop. True. I wanted to think it hadn't happened before and it wouldn't happen again. True. He was good at convincing me. He said he was a traditional kind of guy. He said he wanted a family. True true true. He said there would be no need for me to continue working, that I could if I wished, but there would be no need. It was my decision. False.

He loved me, Dr. Hoffman. Don't you know that? He really, really, really, really loved me.

What? I have a visitor?

I place the test booklet on the white bed and walk through the white framed doorway behind white-clad Harold.

"Half an hour," he says, and opens the door to a small office, closing it quietly as soon as I am inside. I hear his whistle fade down the hallway.

She seems so much smaller, and she sees that I've observed this about her even before I sit down.

"It's true," she says in greeting, "I'm the incredible shrink-ing woman." She lights a cigarette. "So. How are you?"

I'm wearing a hospital gown, Mother. It's white. So are the pills. I'm very calm. They've got me locked in a small white room where there is constant light and no noise. Just a little experiment in sensory deprivation. I'm having the time of my life. How are you, besides disappearing?

"I'm thinking of moving to New Jersey," she says. "On the coast somewhere."

"I've never thought of Jersey as having a coast," I say. "Except I suppose for Atlantic City."

"I've had quite enough of Texas," she says. "Everyone is so strange."

"Here, too," I say.

"You're in Texas," she says. "Did you forget?"

"This is not Texas," I say. "This is a federal outpost that happens to be located within the state boundaries of Texas. This place is stranger than anyplace you've ever been, Mother, stranger even than your version of Texas. This place is a fucking madhouse."

"Such language," she says.

"Most of the women in here have scars," I say. "If they didn't do it to themselves, someone else, usually a boyfriend or lover, did it for them. They're all so beat up, Mother, so battered, these women, and they just accept it, look at it as inevitable. It's as if we're a traveling freak show that doesn't travel."

"Part of a larger carnival." She smiles. "I think Texas was settled accidentally. Everyone was headed for California. Some people made it. Others only got this far before they were exhausted. So they looked around and said, 'This'll do.' They settled."

She stubs out her cigarette, delicately, carefully, neatly.

"Are you treated well?"

"I'm not here for treatment, although the doctor seems to be interested in trying. I'm just sort of . . . here. They're observing. I was in the middle of a test when they told me I had a visitor. I wasn't expecting to see anyone."

"Oh," she says. "I've interrupted."

"Actually it's a relief, I guess."

"You guess."

"Yes."

"I'll let you get back, then," she says, hurt and relieved at once. She's wearing a neat cotton suit. Navy blue skirt and jacket. White wrinkleless blouse. Accessorized.

She kisses the air next to my cheek. She doesn't know what to say.

"You know" — she turns back — "women simply didn't leave their husbands in those days. It wasn't done. I didn't know any better."

"Mother," I say.

"I could have told you," she says. "You were never much at listening. But I could have told you."

Told me what.

"About him," she says. "I know the type. They're everywhere. Specially in Texas. I could have told you."

Nobody could have told me.

I didn't even tell her about the wedding until after the arrangements were made, the invitations in the mail. Until it was too late for her to attempt seriously to talk me out of it. Perhaps because I knew she would try.

She was at home that afternoon, as usual. One thing I'll say for my father, he paid his premiums, even if it cut into his bar tab. Once he was gone, she had no obligations. Her days and nights were her own.

That Sunday, I left Daniel tinkering with his airplane and

went to visit. Fort Worth and Dallas were about equidistant from Rancho Milagro, but she had left Fort Worth within a few months of my father's death. She didn't want Cowtown; she wanted Big D.

I let myself in and stood for a long quiet moment just inside the living room, a million miles away from where she was curled up on the couch, the crossword in her lap, a Bloody Mary in her hand, cigarette in the ashtray, burning, unsmoked, forgotten. Her needs were seemingly met, or at least kept at bay, when she had her puzzles and Bloody Marys. She's adept, able to blitz through the Sunday *New York Times* puzzle (the only reason she subscribes) in twenty to thirty minutes.

She waited until I sat down across from her, in the chair that was "mine" all through childhood and beyond, the matching one next to it empty, before looking up and noticing her abandoned cigarette.

"What a surprise," she said mildly. "You don't happen to know a nine-letter word for 'unsay,' do you?"

"Let me think about it. But I have something to tell you."

"You're pregnant," she said.

"No, Mother," I told her. "But I'm getting married."

"Oh, Cynthia," she said, looking at her puzzle, "you don't really want to have children, do you? Not yet. You still have so much to . . ."

She shrugged. I sat there. I hadn't really expected her to be happy. I hadn't expected.

"I'm thirty-two. I'm ready to settle down."

"But you've always been very settled," she said. "It's not as if you ran away from home and did that Haight-Ashbury thing." She half-laughed. "I just don't want to see you tied down to a bunch of screaming kids before you're ready. It's

real work, you know; it's terribly, terribly hard, raising children. You never have a minute."

"Was it that awful, Mother? Raising us? Were we that
terrible?"

"Oh" — she smiled, returning to her puzzle — "you
know what I mean. I was very fond of you and your sister.
I thought the world of you kids. All I'm saying is that it's a
lot more difficult than you could ever imagine. I'm only
saying that you might want to wait awhile. And you don't
really know this Daniel, do you now? You could take some
time."

"Repudiate," I said.

"What?"

"The word you're looking for. Does it start with R? It
might be 'repudiate.' "

"So it is," she said. "Thank you." She filled in the
squares with her impeccable lettering. "You know, Cynthia," she said, "that if you really think you're ready, I'll say
fine. I just don't want you coming back here asking why I
didn't try to explain what you were getting into. I don't
guess I *can* explain it really. But I think you could take a few
months, or a few years, and not be the worse for the wait."

"You don't know what it's been like," I said. "I've done
everything I set out to do. Graduated with honors, made a
career, got a great apartment and made lots of friends. But,
Mother, I have to tell you, the whole time, something big
was missing. I met Daniel and found out what it was. We
want children. We want a family."

She sipped her drink and replaced it on its coaster.

"It's only your body talking, dear, expressing God only
knows whatever kind of genetic programming's locked up
inside us. All I'm saying is that you should permit your

mind to function as well. Think about what you're thinking about. You've heard of PMS?"

"Of course," I said.

"Well, PMS is your body's way of telling you that if you, yes *you*, don't get pregnant right this instant, and I mean *now*, the entire human race will simply disappear from the face of the earth."

"I've thought, Mother. I really have. Daniel and I want to have a family."

"Well, then" — she sighed, returning once again to her crossword — "you should think some more."

I have no defense. But I know how I felt in those weeks before Daniel and I married. I know I looked forward to each day. I looked forward to a future. While it was happening, while I was looking forward, I was the happiest I've ever been.

"Take care of yourself," Mother says now. "You're looking thin. You need to eat. I suppose the food isn't much."

"Jim Jones would've loved it."

"Well," she says, "I'll let you get back."

I follow Harold back down the hall and picture exactly how I will tell Dr. Hoffman about my mother's visit. Doctor, I will say, it went just like this:

She gave me the biggest hug you could imagine and her smile was so full of love that I was filled with remembrances of childhood happiness. She told me that she was working hard to get me out of here, that she had an attorney on the case and that she expected news just any day. She said she knew we would win. But in the meantime, how could she help? Did I need anything? Anything at all?

Yes, doctor, she really said it, just that way. It was such a relief.

Can I go home now?

Harold shuts the door. I pick up the booklet.

At elections I find myself voting for men about whom I know next to nothing.

Almost always true. *True.*

I used to like Mother May I.

True. *True.*

I would like to hunt elephants in Africa.

I am not afraid of spiders.

My face has not been paralyzed.

My skin is unusually sensitive to touch.

I run from facing a crisis.

I would like to be a cobbler.

I am afraid of using a knife or any other sharp object.

I put down the test booklet, surrounded by white.

Doctor, I will say, it went just like this:

I didn't think I was God, I didn't think anything. I took steps to stop the blows, the crack of Daniel's fists against my skin. I watched from seventh row center the arteries begging for the cut, bulging, ripe with need, saw the instant flash of sharpened steel gleaming, blinding, glaring, the knife opening him beautifully, with the instantaneous precision of indifference well nurtured, cultivated, worked at over time. The knife opened his skin, let drain with gorgeous despair the red of him, the blood of him, *red and red and red and more.* I gave Daniel the thing he needed desperately, the thing he had asked for from the start, from the first kiss, from the first time he raised his fist. I was merciful, I loved him, I caressed his neck. His skin needed the blade. I let him go. I *survived.*

My lawyer wears a tastefully cut skirt instead of trousers, her dark brown hair pulled back tight against her head and knotted at the neck. A bow instead of a tie. Heels, but not heels, of shined black leather. The uniform. I respect this. She has donned the proper armor. In spite of it, she is an attractive woman.

We sit in the examining room, which is attached to Dr. Hoffman's office. I've not been here since the day I entered, whenever that was, but I know it's been more than the estimated six weeks, and am surprised at this physical reminder that Dr. Hoffman is, in fact, under the law, a medical doctor. I rest atop the examining table, arms dangling off either side. I've been given a pair of khakis and a white T-shirt for her visit. U.S. Government military hand-me-downs. The paper that runs down the center of the black artificial leather table top is white. But it's soft up here, and there are colors and sounds in this room.

My lawyer, yes, mine. I hired her because the police said I had the right to remain silent. I was already in handcuffs by then. They came for me at Rancho Milagro and took me to Daniel's body. A polite and seersuckered federal agent read me the warning, and I remember thinking, 'My God, I've been silent too long, that's why we're all standing here,' and how absurd such a thought was, and they had covered the body by then, and I remember the light blue stripes on the agent's suitcoat screaming at me, pleading with me to talk, but I remained silent.

My lawyer sits on the little black stool that usually belongs to Dr. Hoffman. I wish I knew her better. She seems capable and well-spoken, completely composed, but I have not yet been able to locate her spirit.

"He hasn't given me much," she says. "He claims you're not cooperating in the least. He says you've suffered a setback of some kind."

"Absolutely not true," I say calmly. "He claims I broke

down? Absurd. None of this has anything to do with any kind of reality that I've ever known, and, I mean, Ms. Cohen —"

"Please," she interrupts. "Debra."

"Debra. The man is a shrink in a federal prison. Doesn't that just about say it? I'll tell you the truth. I cannot begin to describe the incompetence; I cannot deal with this much incompetence. Have you ever taken the Minnesota Multiphasic Personality Inventory? Have you ever taken the notorious ink blot test? This is science? I don't think so. Have you ever really conversated with the doctor?"

She looks nonplussed.

"Conversated?"

"Excuse me, I meant to say conversed. Have you ever conversed with the doctor?"

"Do you usually go on like this?" she asks. "Do you do this with Dr. Hoffman?"

"I don't think so. I try not to." Was I ranting? I pull at my T-shirt. Soft. Did I stutter? "It's just that room," I say. "Where he keeps me. I haven't had a chance to talk to anyone for a while. I need out of there. Can you file a writ or something?"

"I understand." She makes a note. "Look," she says, writing, "I don't have any more respect for this guy than you do, but he is what we must deal with. And I have to tell you, it's best if you at least seem to cooperate with him."

"But, Debra, I do cooperate. I mean, I know exactly what the man's . . . I know what he's doing. I know exactly what he's doing. He's subjecting me to sensory deprivation. He's torturing me. Do you understand? I'm dealing with it because I know what he's up to. I take his inane little tests, I stay in that maddening room without making a peep, I am courteous and well behaved. I would even say I interact well with my fellow inmates, when permitted to do so. I eat the food."

"Cynthia."

"*Mizzzzz* Cohen. I am not insane. I am perfectly capable of understanding the charges against me. Believe me, no one understands the charges against me the way I do. I am aware of the possible consequences of those charges. And, if given the opportunity, I am quite capable of assisting in my defense. Are not those the criteria?"

"Indeed. You've forgotten only one thing."

"Yes?"

"I'm on your side."

9 My lawyer has managed to keep her word. Dr. Hoffman came this morning and stood angrily in the white room but contained his anger, permitted it to show only briefly before saying, "I've decided it's time for you to return. I think, though, that putting you back with Emma would be a mistake."

The white room around him was blinding me, but my hands behaved themselves all the while he was there. I began to wonder if perhaps they were considering coming back to life.

"I mean after all," he said, "you're here to deal with your own situation, but you don't seem willing to do that while you have Emma's problems to distract you. So I'm putting you in with Elizabeth."

Kissy's wearing her red dress again, modeling it for me in the middle of our room as she quietly hums "Hello, Dolly." I haven't yet told her that I know her real name.

She looks good in the dress. It's a strapless number that shows off her figure, and her figure, though too buxom for today's magazine covers, is great. She, however, is convinced that her thighs are overwhelming.

"I never wore this on the street," she says. "It just hung in my closet. But one Sunday morning there I was sleeping peacefully in my bed and someone bangs on the door, they didn't even use the doorbell for God's sake, and the next thing I know my little niece, who was three and had come for the weekend, is standing next to my bed saying, 'Aunt Kissy, wake up, the *minigrashumens* are here. They want to talk to you.'"

She twirls once lightly and sits on her bed, which is next to the window, like the one I used to sleep on when I roomed with Emma.

"Immigration," she says. "It was the *immigration mens*. You see, I had this little scheme going to assist Asian immigrants. Just a quiet method of speeding the process for those who wished to enter the good old U. S. of A. and happened to have a little disposable income lying around. Frankly, I don't understand why they had to make such a big deal out of the whole affair. The prosecutor accused me of subverting the fabric of the United States of America. I mean, get real. Anyone asks what I'm in for, I should tell them I'm a fabric subverter?"

"And why Veritas?"

"Oh, who knows," she says. "I was just miserable out there on the main compound. They call this dump a country club? I don't see anyone on the wait list for membership, sweetheart. I mean *quelle* squalor! Who could deal with it? It's hot, it's noisy, it's unbelievably overcrowded. It's smelly, the food is absolutely rotten and no one has the first idea of what courtesy is. It's poorly ventilated, for God's sake. So about my third week in I said to myself, 'Why not go crazy?' I'd heard there was air conditioning over here. *Voilà.* I am, as they say, crazy like a fox."

I'm not sure, but I think she's telling the truth.

"And don't try ratting me out to the doc," she says. "I'll only deny I ever said it."

"Wouldn't dream of it," I say. "Where you wish to stay is your business. It doesn't make any difference to me." Nothing makes any difference to me now except that I am out of the white room, off Two, back where I belong.

"Oh, Cynthia" — she pretends to whine — "and here I thought we were going to be friends."

"We can be," I say. "But just don't go accusing me of things I haven't done."

"I wasn't accusing you of anything. Juh-he-zus H. Keerist. I was only telling you not to tell Hoffman. I was just a little nervous that I'd told you how I got here."

"It's okay," I tell her. I don't say that I wasn't talking about that. She doesn't know I was talking about killing Alice. I cannot bear to hear one more person accuse me of killing my sister.

"Anyway," she says, "I used to have these great pumps that match this dress exactly. They took them away from me when I arrived at this hellhole. Said they were confiscating them because they could be used as weapons."

"How high were the heels?"

"Oh, honey. To die for. I mean, to die for. Some kind of gorgeous-looking spikes. Four inches maybe?"

"And you wore them to jail?"

"You bet. The marshals were kind enough to wait in the living room while I changed out of my favorite flannel bunny jammies. One of them almost fell over when I finally walked out. I was dressed to the nines, evening make-up, Valentino handbag, the works. It was seven-thirty on a Sunday morning."

"And your niece? What did she think about all this?" I'm not even sure why we're having this conversation, except that I'm beginning to suspect that Kissy lives in her own special reality, and that her relationship with the truth is somewhat tenuous. But she's doing a fine job of making things up.

"My niece was okay with it," she says. "It was my sister. When I called to tell her she had to come get her daughter, I thought she was going to have a cow."

We sit in silence for a moment, adjusting to being in the same room, trying to figure out what it feels like to be in this place together, wondering how well, if at all, we will get along. No less an entity than the United States Government has plucked the two of us from our separate lives and thrown us together here in Veritas. It almost seems as though we no longer exist outside the confines of this room.

I sit staring at the window, the darkness behind the green wire mesh, and remember how, on the occasional trip to my grandparents' house in south Texas, the road led us past the big state prison outside Huntsville. Even on the sunniest autumn days, as we flew past in the station wagon on our way to Thanksgiving, I would cringe as we neared the place. I remember even now, especially now, how forbidding it was and how I thought, as a little girl, that it must be full of monsters, full of terrible, awful, murderous, rabid, horrible human beings. I held my breath as the car entered into what I thought was the realm of the prison, held it for the interminably long moments it took to drive past the high brick walls, past the chain link, past the concertina wire with its razor barbs glinting hungrily in the sun. Past the gun towers that held frightening human-shaped silhouettes. I was afraid to breathe lest I catch some pernicious virus that must surely be lurking in the air, trapped in the gigantic, invisible bell jar that I was certain hung over the prison like a shroud. I could not imagine what it must be like to be in that place. It was not real.

It still isn't. Or it is too real, I'm not sure which. Kissy and I and every other inmate in here, all of us, have exited the larger world. Out there somewhere, beyond the walls of this institution, people eat, sleep, work and sometimes manage to think for a few minutes or play or spend time with those they love. Those who knew us may have moments of sadness when they think of where we are; it's almost as if we have died. It is painful for them to think of where we are. They try not to. The world spins on, having never noticed that any of us were part of it. It is truly, this business of being locked up, much like having a good long look at things from the other side of the grave.

"C'mon," Kissy says suddenly. "It's time for Coffee's reading."

I follow her down the hallway and we sit next to each other on the couch. We will become friends. We will make the best of things.

At first I think it is because of Kissy, but soon I realize that they're not looking at her at all. They're stealing long strange looks at me. I focus on Coffee and pretend not to notice anything or anyone else. Glenda has blue and green scarves tied around her wrists and is trying to show Three Sheets how the new beauty marks on her stomach have popped out in the shape of a crab.

"It's a very, like, nurturing sign," she says seriously. "You know, everyone thinks that the sign for Cancer is like sixty-nine turned sideways, but it's not at all. It represents the breasts and it represents that what is given is not lost. It represents, among other things, because you know this is a very complicated discipline, but one of the things it represents is motherhood. Like wow. Really. You know, Three Sheets, don't you, that the love you give away doesn't actually, like, leave you. I mean it leaves, but it stays too. Like, you give it away but more grows in its place so you actually get love every time you give love away. I mean, like, what I'm trying to say is whatever love you give to others remains within you also and makes you grow, you know, it like nurtures you, makes your spirit grow, like it increases your vital force."

Nina leans over to whisper, "Ground control to Major Mom. Like, wow, you know, positively cosmic. I'd just like to know what kind of booster rocket the wench used to launch herself into orbit." At least Nina is not staring at me. At least she's talking to me as if I'm a normal, ordinary human being.

"But Nina," I say, "isn't that the same stuff our man Sigmund was talking about? You know, libido and all that? What would Dr. Hoffman think if he heard you talking like this?"

"Yeah," she says, "what would he think? But Freud, don't you know, put a believable spin on it all."

"Freud was a cokehead," Kissy says. "He was full of shit."

"Yeah," Nina says, "but he created an industry. And look at us now. Know what I mean, Jelly Bean?"

Three Sheets slides her swollen hand reverently along the blue and green chiffons tied to Glenda's wrists.

"Can I wear these some time?" she asks.

"After July twenty-second," Glenda responds, "I'll let you have them for keeps. I'll *give* them to you."

"Why July twenty-second?"

"Do you always look a gift horse in the mouth?" Glenda asks. "Can't you just accept graciously?"

Three Sheets doesn't seem to get it. I empathize.

"We'll be in Leo then," Glenda says nastily, "whose colors are orange and gold."

Coffee has prepared herself and turns to face the camera. She recites:

> A cloudy sky,
> cat guts on pitted pavement,
> raindrop in my eye,
> thunder in my mind,
> and a big, big question
> that nobody wants to answer.
> It's Monday and I'm halfway there.
> Bastards locked my ass up
> for not such a long time,
> least not, girlfriend, for
> such a serious crime.
> I do okay.
> Not really living
> never quite dying

time easin' on by
but it always keep easin'.
Evenings, the scent of yesterday
comes over the wall on the breeze.
And I'll give you the what-for, honey.
It smells like tomorrow to me.

Nina's hand shakes slightly as she lights her cigarette.

"Hey, Slick," Coffee says, "where'd you score the fire?"

"That was very real, Coffee," Nina says. "You got real on that one. I liked that. I hope you do more like that one."

"Good enough," Coffee says. "I appreciate your appreciation."

"She shows promise," Kissy says. I'm not sure, from the tone of her voice, if she's serious.

"I should know," she adds. "I used to teach English." To me, "Up in your neck of the woods."

"Where at?"

"Columbia University."

"No kidding," I say, but I'm sure she is. "When was this?"

"A few years ago. I said *hasta la vista* after I was denied tenure. The English department there is controlled by the PLO. They weren't up to having a woman in their ranks, much less a Jewish woman."

Nina is pretending to enjoy her cigarette, but I know she's soaking up every word.

"Was this before or after the immigration thing?" I ask.

"During, actually. That was only a sideline."

"So what were you doing when they arrested you?"

"I told you already. I was watching my niece."

"Occupationally."

"Oh, I was between gigs, you know. I'd left the university about a month earlier. I was considering taking some acting classes, something that would be, you know, another piece of gâteau entirely."

"This one," Coffee announces, "is called 'Give and Take.' " She takes her stance. I can picture her in the same pose, her feet spread wide, her legs poised to run, as she stands in a convenience store holding a pistol in a shaking clerk's face. Though I would never let her know it, I'd be terrified to meet Coffee out in the real world. "On the streets" they call it in here. I would not want to meet Coffee on the streets. Her poem comes out like a sneer.

"It is the big thump boomer," she begins, and goes on to speak of robbing banks, robbing drug stores, being a prostitute, being an addict, stealing cars, kiting checks and her favorite — the time she and her crew stole a prisoner transport bus from in front of the Metropolitan Correction Center in Miami. While it was full of prisoners.

". . . stuffing your own lungs with wonder," Coffee continues, "and hoping to see a hero bleed."

She bows her head to thank us for our attention.

"Wow," Glenda says. "Like, totally macho, man. I was, like, really scared there for a minute."

"Coffee," Kissy says, "or perhaps you wouldn't mind if I called you Café, I think the second one needs a little work." To me she says, "And the poet needs a little work too. Like, some serious therapy."

Coffee wads up her poems and throws them at Kissy.

"Why don't you try them with a little hot fudge," she taunts. "Then maybe you'd get something out of the experience, Miss B-L-U-N-T. Who the fuck you think you are, waltzing in here and telling me I need therapy? Stupid bitch. Psychoanalysis is nothing but more of the white man's bullshit! All those dickhead doctors be namin' names to tell what it is they say be wrong with all their hosehead patients. Mental disorder? Disorders, girl? It comes down to . . ."

Kissy stands as if to leave.

"Wait up, girlfriend," Coffee says, and the honesty in her voice compels Kissy to sit back down. "It's like this. Be nice to people, hold down a job, have a family and love your family. If you can't understand why babies goin' to bed hungry and twelve-year-olds shootin' each other on the street, then there must be something bad wrong wich you.

"Now listen up, sister. I don't need some asshole shrink to tell me that because I choose to fight the power I'm crazy. Because I know what I am. And I'll tell you this, honey. I am not crazy. I'm fuckin' mad."

None of us knows what to say. Kissy stands turned halfway toward the stairwell, clearly wanting to leave, but uncertain whether she can without getting chased down by Coffee. She looks at the ceiling for a moment, then straight at Coffee.

"You're right," she says. "I apologize. I had no business. I apologize."

Coffee seems taken aback by Kissy's sudden turn from sarcasm to straightforwardness.

"All right then," she stammers. "All right. It's cool then." She smiles uncertainly, as though it is an expression she's not at all used to. I think it is the only time I've seen her smile. She has a nice smile that, although not easy, is definitely genuine. It looks good on her.

Kissy smiles back as she heads for the stairs. I wait until Harold slobbers into the room and takes the tape from Coffee before I walk toward my room.

When I get there, the lights are out and Kissy is in bed. I take my bag of toiletries and walk back down the hall to the bathroom. I could stay and wash in the stainless steel unit in the corner of the room, but the water isn't much more than a trickle, and the design of the unit requires that you stand and lean across the toilet in order to reach the sink above it. Altogether awkward. Intentional, I'm sure. Anyone who would choose to design a prison or any part of its interior furnishings can, on the face of that evidence alone, be considered a sadist.

There is a line for the shower, three women standing wrapped in towels, holding their soap and tapping their feet, leaning against the cold tile wall and dreaming of a private bath. I go to one of three sinks against the opposite wall and begin washing my face.

It doesn't happen often, but when it does, when it happens, it is all I can do not to fall down. It happens when there is water running, or when the radio goes static, when there is white noise, covering noise of any kind, noise that can hide danger. It happens when I close my eyes to rinse my face and cannot see and cannot hear over the noise of the running water. I lean over the sink to rinse my skin, and there he is. I can feel him. Behind me. He has no name. Coming closer. He is always armed, I do not know what with. Something sharp. Or something heavy. Something that will take my head off. He stands behind me as I wash. He has no name.

I am still shaking when I climb quietly into bed. Kissy sleeps on her back, her arms straight against her sides, the covers tucked neatly under her armpits. Tonight, I go fetal, curl my back against the night, pull my knees up and wrap my arms around them so that I can protect my soft parts, cover my vulnerable belly. I clutch my watch and begin the vigil that will last until daylight seeps up to the edge of the window.

It is an oddly quiet night. Usually someone is snoring or singing or whistling or crying. The stranger cannot get near me now. I would hear his approach. I would be ready for his murderous intentions. The woolen blanket is a shield against whoever or whatever would harm me. I assure myself. Kissy's presence, too, makes it less likely that he, whoever he is, will venture near.

Before Veritas, I would have been uncomfortable sleeping in the same room with a stranger, but now it feels not only normal but comforting. Things will be all right with Kissy. I admire the way she responded to Coffee, undoing the humiliation, erasing it with candor. So far, I like her. I wonder if that means I expect, at some point, not to like her anymore. Perhaps I expect her to change, to reveal a side of her personality that would cause her to take pleasure in trying to hurt me. I wonder if she will live up to my expectations.

Dr. Hoffman would probably accuse me of reading too much into it. He would say it is not Kissy at all who will ultimately prove untrustworthy.

10

I have no doubt that Glenda will be bright red by dinnertime. She has been out there for hours now, her face bare under the July sun. I saw her when I took lunch, such as it was, in my room. And she is there now, trying to get in a few quick pirouettes before trudging upstairs for the four o'clock count. The hacks are already here, milling near the end of the hall, clipboards in hand, eager to pester their captives.

I did two hundred and seven mailbags today, my hands

alive throughout. I hope Dr. Hoffman is keeping track of my productivity.

Glenda traipses down the hall to 305 just as a towheaded young hack with the twangiest Texas accent I have ever heard begins the count. He looks a little like Clint Eastwood with blond hair. Nina, I can see, is impressed. When she thinks no one is looking, she loosens the neckline of her bathrobe just a tad, just enough to display a hint of cleavage. When the hack stops at 304 to ask Emma where her roommate is, I get Nina's attention and mouth the words "Shameless hussy," which brings a smile to her face and encourages her to slouch into a prostitute lean against the doorframe.

Emma doesn't respond to the hack; she merely looks past him to where I stand in front of 310, next to Janna's room, almost directly across the hall.

"I'm over here," I say to him. "Behind you."

He turns slowly and puts one hand on his hip.

"That's a shot," he says. "I'm gonna write you up."

"I am exactly where I'm supposed to be," I say. "Dr. Hoffman moved me here."

"You must be new," Nina says, hitting him with the inmate's strongest weapon against a guard: You're the new kid, you don't know how it works around here. And you're probably scared shitless.

"She hasn't even been on this hall for the last three weeks," Nina says, smiling. "She's been downstairs on Two. This is only her second day back. So you can go ahead and write her up, give her a shot, but it won't stick. She's telling the truth."

I don't think Nina particularly wants to defend me against him, but she does want his attention. Was I really in the white room for three weeks? She probably wants more than his attention. Kissy stands quietly next to me, nibbling on a bright red fingernail to keep herself from laughing as she watches the exchange. Where did she get the nail polish?

"Was I really in the white room for three whole weeks?" I whisper to her.

"Honey," she says, "I don't know from any white room, but you sure weren't here. Nothing personal, you understand, but I did enjoy my privacy."

The young blond fellow one-two-threes his way past Herlinda, Coffee, Nina, Janna, makes a big show of crossing my name off one spot on his list and writing it in another, passes Kissy and me and counts his way back around to the entrance to A Hall.

"Remain in your rooms until the count is cleared," he announces, then stomps off with Officer Svejk lolling behind, shaking his head slowly, amused by all the fuss.

Nina fans her face with one hand, feigning a swoon, and then half rolls, half falls, through the doorway to 308. I follow Kissy into 310 and we take up our places on our beds.

"Gosh," Kissy says sarcastically, "she must really think he's cute."

We sit waiting for the count to clear.

"You know," she says suddenly, "I've got a stash of Aztec secret."

"Feel free," I say, "but I don't do drugs."

"It's Indian healing clay." She laughs. "You use it for a facial, for God's sake. Should we do one while we wait?" She goes into her locker and comes out with a plastic bag full of pale green powder. "This stuff is incredible," she says. "You won't believe how good your skin will feel. Don't ask me how I got the apple cider vinegar." She mixes the clay and vinegar, which turn into dark green foam, and begins stroking it onto my cheeks and forehead, then down on my neck. She hands me the plastic cup in which she has mixed the ingredients, and I paint a dark green mask on her face. Up close, I see that she has a layer of very light freckles scattered across her nose and cheeks. Her eyes are palest blue, almost gray, and look startling once I've surrounded them with green.

We lie back on our beds. The mud is cool and soothing at first; then it begins to dry and tighten, pulling the pores of my skin closed, tingling. It gives me a clean feeling, something I haven't often had since coming to Veritas.

"By the way," Kissy says, "I've started an aerobics class."

"Here?"

"No, Cynthia, they let us out for field trips now. Didn't anyone tell you?"

"When does it meet?"

"Monday Wednesday Friday. Ten to eleven A.M. There's one tomorrow. First-floor dayroom. Be there or be round."

"What music do we work out to?" I ask.

"We warm up to 'Folsom Prison Blues,' " she smiles. "Then there's Elvis, of course, 'Jailhouse Rock.' And that other one, 'I Fought the Law.' Who did that?"

"I don't have a clue. No Beatles? No Stones? No Kinks?"

"British is your thing, then?"

"I don't know."

"So who was your favorite Beatle?" she asks.

For a moment it's as though I'm back in college, with Kissy as my roommate. It's Friday evening and we've decided to stay in the dorm and pamper ourselves.

"John," I say.

"God, Cyn," she says, "that's pretty weird. Every self-respecting female I knew went for Paul. John Lennon?"

"What can I say, Kiss?" I sigh. "There was something about him that intrigued me. I couldn't defend my choice way back then, not even to my sister, who was only four at the time but appalled that I liked him, and I had almost three years on her when we discovered them one night on Ed Sullivan." I stop suddenly, realizing I've slipped, I've let her trap me. Was she trying to trap me? She's there on her bed, staring at the ceiling, not really paying attention. Maybe she didn't notice.

But she did. She takes her time sitting up.

"Why, Cynthia," she says slowly, her voice full of mock astonishment, "I didn't know you had a sister. What's her name? Where does she live? Tell me all about her. I mean, who knows" — she sweeps an arm around the room — "we could be here for hours while that little creep learns how to count."

"Kissy," I say, careful not to stutter, "it's not something I want to talk about. My sister has been dead for some time now. I loved her. I did not kill her. That's all I want to say about it. Right now, I think I'll just close my eyes until they release us for dinner."

She lets herself fall back on the bed and props her feet up against the wire mesh over the window.

"I'm sorry, Cyn," she says sincerely. "I didn't mean to bring up something like that. I was just making conversation, you know. I didn't even dream that something like that had happened. I thought it was just a Cuban rumor, you know, all that *quien mató blah-blah-blah.* How did she die? What happened to her?"

"Elizabeth," I say — her eyes widen with surprise — "I

really don't want to talk about it. It wasn't my fault. That's all I have to say." I feel as if I'm choking. "So." Am I stuttering? "Could we just not talk about it?" I close my eyes and feel the mud on my face throbbing, taut now and dry, starting to burn. I hear Kissy get up and rinse her mask off in the pathetic dribble of water from the sink in the corner of our room. I roll to face the wall and lie silently, squeezing back tears I thought weren't there, concentrating on now, on this moment falling into the next, each taking me farther from the memory, and so farther from the knowledge, and so farther from culpability.

Herlinda is carrying a large stack of finished mailbags to the trolley and we almost collide as I round the corner into the workroom.

"Gringita!" she cries. "Watch where you're going, will you?" She balances her way to the trolley and dumps her stack of bags on top of what's already there.

Hundreds of them. Hundreds upon hundreds. I imagine them filled with mail: pen pal letters, bills, catalogues, special offers, smelly little perfume promos, junk junk junk. Love letters?

Zillions of bags every day, filled with mail. All those postal workers lugging all that paper around. How many tons? Good news. Bad or indifferent news. No news at all, just another one-day sale for just another Special Customer.

I wrote letters after I moved to Texas to be with Daniel. My friends were all in New York, and I wrote regularly at first. When I didn't hear back, I stopped. I knew how it was in the city, so I let it rest. It was not until after Daniel was gone that I found them. Letters addressed to me, from my friends, tucked away in his desk.

"Earth to Cynthia," I hear Herlinda saying. She guides me to my place at the work table. I can do this. My hands are functional today. I pick up a piece of rope.

Herlinda whispers, "So it's true?"

I know immediately what she's talking about. Kissy has wasted no time in spreading the word.

But Kissy has it wrong. Herlinda has it wrong. And so everyone else in the unit will have it wrong.

She was the one who swallowed the pills.

I was the one who found her. Only hours later. The skin of the dead. I understand full well when the priests say it in Mass: dear departed souls. I know what a body looks like when the soul has departed. Some of them still manage to walk and talk and eat and sleep and go to their jobs for years and years, long after their souls have departed. But my sister was not one of them.

She liked to feed people; she liked to cook huge, wonderful meals and gather friends around her table. Eventually she opened her own small place just outside Dallas in an enormous old barn that had been converted into an offbeat shopping mall. Everything sold there was hand-made: quilts, clothing, candles, furniture. Ali's was the only restaurant, and people lined up daily for the home-cooked lunches, especially for her soups.

Though I never told her, I knew Alice was one of those rare beings who saw goodness in every living thing. She loved nature; she loved the human race. She said one afternoon that she thought she might be hiding from all that is ugly and evil in the world by maintaining a permanent state of naïveté. I think that may have made things easier for Daniel.

She was kind enough to leave a note. But she didn't do it

to hurt anyone or try to get even. She was only trying to explain.

She thought it was coincidence. The first time, at a stoplight, he'd only tapped the horn and waved. Some weeks later, at the grocery store checkout counter, he inspected the contents of her shopping cart and approved. And much later, months later, in the big vacant field north of the lake, where she would let her Labradors run in the afternoons, he'd said, "What a surprise . . . just out for some air . . . How wonderful to see you." They went for ice cream.

A few weeks after that he ran into her, early in the evening, at a service station where she'd stopped after realizing suddenly that she was almost out of gas. She thought she'd filled up only a day or two earlier. "We're family," he said. "We should get to know each other," he said. He told her I was working late that night, out with a client. "How about dinner?" he said.

"You don't answer," Herlinda says.

I continue to thread the ropes through the holes in the bags. I concentrate on the details. I smell canvas and metal; the scent of floor polish rises up from the beige linoleum; Svejk's cigarette smoke wafts through the door and floats upward, spreads into the corners of the small workroom and hangs in the quiet air like a blanket suspended a few inches from the ceiling. For some reason I usually think of him as guarding us. Which is stupid of me. He's guarding them. He is guarding society. We are the ones he is protecting against.

There was no one to protect me from Daniel. No one to protect my sister from Daniel or from herself. Where were all the guards?

Perhaps if my father had still been alive. That thought is gone before I can finish it. I could see it. Excuse me, Dad, you know all those times you whacked Mom around? Well, my husband, Daniel, is doing the same thing to me. Would you please tell him to stop, please?

"Gringa," Herlinda says, "you look bad again. You look that way again."

I slow myself down. I bring myself back to the room.

"It's okay, Herlinda. Thank you. I'm all right."

"You would feel so much better if you would talk about it."

"I don't think I can."

"Gringita," she says, smiling, "you can do whatever you decide to do. If you don't want to, you don't want to. That is your decision. But say you don't want to; don't say you can't."

"Herlinda," I say carefully, "I hope to be able to talk about it at some point. But I don't want to right now."

I hadn't realized that the passivity Daniel demanded became so much a part of me that it crept into my language. I foreshortened my vocabulary to give the illusion that I needed him, the illusion that he loved me. And the passivity that he forced on me became embedded in the way I think, deleted certain words from my language. I have forgotten how to use words of choice, words of decision. I absolve myself from responsibility by saying "I can't" when I mean "I don't want to." This frightens me. How insidious it was. How easily it happened.

"That's fine," Herlinda says. "I hope soon you will talk about it." She picks up another mailbag and returns to her work.

At ten o'clock I show my pass to Officer Svejk and go down the hall to the dayroom.

Kissy has on full aerobic regalia. She is in spandex from

shoulder to ankle. A jumpsuit of black and aqua. Matching tennis shoes. Matching headband and wristbands. She has done her nails, too, in a diagonal pattern — half black, half aqua. I love this woman's attitude.

Coffee has chosen more subdued attire. She has on green fatigue pants tucked into thick black socks and bloused about her ankles. Her plain white T-shirt has been cut into a bra-high fringe and elaborately knotted. She wears a tightly twisted black-and-white paisley kerchief around her head, and black weightlifting gloves, the kind with the fingers cut out. I love this woman's attitude, too.

Glenda has on her usual half-hippy, half-ballerina outfit, but has traded in her toe shoes for a pair of purple Converse high-tops.

The rest of us, except for Nina, are in assorted combinations of sweats and Ts. I'm glad I brought tennis shoes to jail. Nina positions herself at arm's length to my left. She is still wearing her blue bathrobe and slippers.

"I'll be fine," she says to me, answering my look. She raises what's left of one eyebrow. She has plucked her brows so that they are less than an eighth of an inch wide and not even long enough to curve, like miniature Mr. Spock eyebrows, only blond.

Kissy presses a button on the tape player she has borrowed from Dr. Hoffman and pulls herself up into the first stretch of her routine.

"Okay, now, ladies," she says, "let's get loose here, let's get into this, I want you to really reach, reach for the ceiling. We're gonna work out seriously here, we're gonna raise a sweat. Don't think of it as prison aerobics; think of it as getting in shape so you too can escape."

She reaches and turns up the volume and we all copy her

stretch as we hear the opening notes of "Don't Cry for Me, Argentina."

He has my father's eyes. Some days he has my father's mouth, too. I can't believe I hadn't noticed the similarity. The drawn lips, the slightly angry, downturned corners. There are no laugh lines on Dr. Hoffman's face.

"Tell me," he says now, "what exactly it is you hope to get from this experience."

"This experience? What I hope to get?" I cross my legs as he has crossed his. I'm still in my sweats, still sweating from Kissy's murderous workout. Ten o'clock aerobics, eleven o'clock shrink. Good for the body, good for the mind? "The right to stand trial," I tell him.

"But what else?" he asks. "Have you considered the possibility that you might benefit personally from your time in here?"

Seeing him twice a week, seeing him on Friday mornings when he comes into the room and palpates and takes blood pressures and listens to our hearts, and seeing him as I see him today, as he sits behind his desk and fixes his Wednesday-morning gaze on me, seeing him, being around him, becoming familiar with him, these things make me want to trust him. I know it's only because he's here, because he pretends to listen or perhaps sometimes really does listen, that I want to talk to him. But to convince him of my competence, I will have to communicate, and without trust, there can be no communication, so I am back where I started: sitting here watching him look at me and wondering if he sees a lunatic.

"No," I answer honestly, "that hasn't crossed my mind. I would say it's more a case of trying not to let my time in here be detrimental. Let's face it, doctor, Veritas lacks a certain, as Kissy would put it, *je ne sais quoi*."

"How is Kissy?" he asks. "How is that going? Do you two get along?"

"We get along fine, doctor, although we don't necessarily agree on very much. But Kissy is much easier to deal with than Emma. I'll admit, it was depressing to room with her."

"Moods," he says, "are known to be contagious."

"I was vaccinated long ago."

He turns to take a long look out the window behind him; he has a different view of the same brick and chain link and concertina wire that each of us inmates has from her window; he turns again to face me and leans back in his chair and blows air through his lips in a loose sort of whistle.

"So tell me, Cynthia," he says finally, "are we going to spend these sessions in lighthearted banter, or are we going to try to discover how you might, in the future, avoid getting yourself into the kind of mess you find yourself in now? Because regardless of what you may think of me" — and then a confidential aside: "I am, after all, a psychiatrist and I do work in a prison hospital" — he pulls himself forward and says, "but if we can get past that and get past what I'm well aware are your prejudices against me, I think something good could come of this. Understanding, of course, that my primary role is to evaluate you for the court, I still think I may be able to help you. Off the record, of course."

I don't know what to say. He waits.

"In other words," I say, "you want me to continue to believe in the myth of beneficent patriarchy?"

"What is that supposed to mean?"

"It means that, in my opinion, Father may not always know best."

"I agree completely," he says. "But why do you assume that *I want* you to continue to believe in anything? Why do you assume that *I want* anything? Why is what *I want* important to you, Cynthia? Why do you need to please me?"

"I don't need to," I say. "What's important to me is that you understand that I'm able to stand trial and that you'll tell that to the judge."

"That's it?"

"Yes. That's all there is to it."

"You're scheduled for a hearing next week," he says.

I'm glad I'm still sweating from the workout. He cannot see how this news affects me. If my face weren't already red, the flush of fear would show immediately. Though he can't see it, I can certainly feel it.

"What day?" I ask.

"Monday. Nine A.M."

He hands me a pass and sends me back to the workroom. When I sit down, Herlinda waves a hand in front of her face and says, "No shower after your exercise?"

"At lunch," I tell her. "I'll shower at lunch."

"Gringita," she says.

"Herlinda," I say. "It's only fifteen minutes or so. Relax."

We are flying through mailbags when Kissy skids into the room, wild-eyed and breathless.

"You can't believe it," she says, panting. "You can't believe it."

"Tell us," Herlinda says.

"It's Nina," Kissy gasps. "I just heard she's killed herself. Cut her own throat. Cut herself wide open. She found a razor blade, for God's sake. She's done the Big S."

She is back out the door before I can ask where. Where is Nina. Where did she do it. Where did she find the blade.

I hear Herlinda whisper something in Spanish, and then she begins praying softly, turning back to her work as she does. Lulu sits stunned. The others follow Herlinda's lead and go silently back to work.

Svejk sticks a hand in his pocket. I ask if I may go to my room and he slowly shakes his head as he pulls out a cigarette.

"Not now," he says. "We'd all better just stay where we are for the time being. Until I hear from upstairs." He sucks in smoke, tilts his head back, lets it out slowly, watching as it floats toward the ceiling.

The dullness in his face tells me he has seen this before and has learned how not to let it affect him.

11

Tiny moon-shaped slivers of white show at the bottom of Nina's nearly closed eyelids. Beneath the lids, her eyes jump and roll as she dreams, I wonder of what.

The bandages on her wrists shine white in the dark room. I want to wake her, ask her why. Foolish me. I want to grab her by the arms and shake her until an answer falls out of her mouth. A shiver runs through me from head to toe like a low-voltage electric current, leaving me queasy. Her voice echoes in my memory: "Hey, Harold, got a match?" and Harold laughs as he lopes down the hallway with an empty razor in his back pocket, and I close the door of my locker, smug with my deception, the contraband tucked away inside.

From somewhere in this room a voice is telling me that it wasn't my fault. I should argue. I have no desire to argue. I try to assure myself that she would have found something else to do the job. I tell myself I had nothing to do with it. I tell myself it is not my fault.

Just as I told myself with Alice. I cannot bear this. I look at Nina lying on the bed and I see Alice lying on the floor of the kitchen of her restaurant, the place she had made from scratch. All I could hear, in that instant when I realized what she'd done, was the sound of her customers greeting her, the regulars asking what's for lunch, sniffing the aromas from her kitchen and smiling with anticipation. Their hellos became a roar, rumbling through the dark and empty restaurant and filling my head with a noise that I thought surely would burst inside my brain. I could not focus on anything except the earrings she was wearing. They were turquoise, and Daniel had given them to her for Christmas not two months before.

I had seen something that morning, something that fluttered between them when she opened his gift and raised her eyes to thank him. But I'd said to myself it was nothing.

I cannot bear this.

I pull the door shut quietly and walk two doors down. Kissy is awake in the dark.

"Sorry I gave everybody such a fright," she says.

"Rumors," I say, closing the door. "Don't feel bad." Hallway light makes a square of white on the floor, broken with the crisscross shadow of the wire mesh in the glassless window of the door. "Everything in this place gets blown out of proportion, you know? It just happens."

"Anyway," she says, "I'm glad Three Sheets found her. I'm glad she's not dead."

I lie down and fold my hands. I don't want to listen to Kissy right now. But I do not want silence, either.

"Do you know that painting?" I ask. "*The Persistence of Memory?* Clocks draped over things? One hanging off the edge of a cliff?"

"Dali," she says. "Yes."

"Every time I get into this bed I am reminded of that painting. This bed should be in that painting, don't you think? It has that wilting, sagging aspect. It would fit perfectly."

She chuckles. "Did Hoffman take the stitches?" she asks.

"I don't know," I say. "I suppose he must have."

"He's the doctor."

"That's the rumor."

"I felt relieved."

"What?"

"When I did it," she says. "When I tried to do it."

I lie silently, listening.

"It was like this incredible pressure inside my body. I thought I was going to explode. I really thought I was going to blow up. I had to relieve the pressure, and there was only one way to do that."

She turns on her side, props her head on one hand.

"I poured myself a glass of Chablis, got a cigarette, a match and an ashtray, and a razor blade, and I put on Chopin's 'Études.' I locked myself in the bathroom, though I lived alone at that point, and I went into a kind of trance. It didn't hurt. It was as if I were someone else. I wasn't me. Maybe that was it. I needed to know if I was still me. I needed to know where my skin stopped and the world began. I had to check the boundaries."

She falls onto her back.

"But I lacked courage," she says. "I sat there watching myself bleed for a while, actually thinking it was beautiful, the blood in the water, and then I called my shrink. That guy I told you about, the one I fired, Dr. Hank?"

I don't know who she's talking about, but I nod.

"Yeah. I called him. And he was really sweet. He came over and took care of me and put bandages on and all that, and he took me to the hospital and waited while I got stitched up. Then he brought me back to my apartment and asked me if there was anyone I could call. And when I told him no, he said he'd stay with me."

She rolls back up on her elbow.

"Cynthia," she says, "we slept together. That night. That very night. I mean, ask me if I knew what the fuck was going on."

"Kissy," I say, "I'll be back in a few minutes and we can talk some more, okay? I'll be right back."

I leave her there on her bed, looking every bit as dazed as she must have felt that night. I don't know what to say to her. I didn't know what to say to Alice. After Christmas I wondered many times if Daniel had pursued her, if she'd fallen for him, and if he had coaxed or somehow coerced her into bed. There was something in his voice when she called and he answered the phone. And he always answered the phone, telling me not to bother; he'd get it. I suspected, but wouldn't act on my suspicions because I tried always to keep peace in the house. I still don't know how to live with my sister's betrayal. I'll never know how to live with her suicide.

I have convinced myself that I would never try to take my own life. I tell myself that, because I spent several years defending it against Daniel, I cannot understand anyone who would try. But I'm lying. I know what it feels like. Toward the end, I considered it many, many times. I thought about it every day. Some days I thought about it all day. About ending the misery. If I couldn't make myself believe that I had the right to defend myself against him, at least I could tell myself that when it got absolutely too horrible to bear, I could always end it by ending my own life. That was often my consolation. It enabled me to keep breathing.

I duck into 304, where Emma is sleeping as soundly as Nina is in 308. Dr. Hoffman must have broken out some of the heavy stuff. His prescription for Emma's face seems to be doing what it's supposed to do. Her acne is gone. But the skin on her cheeks and chin stays bright red, constantly burned. It looks sore to the touch. Some days it peels. The peeling is so severe that it wouldn't surprise me to find a thin, dried-out layer of skin in the shape of Emma's face lying somewhere in the unit where she'd managed to molt it. But the acne is gone.

I go silently to my old locker, open it with care and am relieved to see the magazines where I left them. I find the *Elle*, find the page with the gorgeous legs, find the depilatory ad.

I do not find the blade.

I sit down slowly, sink down onto the floor, sick and dizzy. My silly game.

Nina might have killed herself. That is all I can think. And then I start telling myself that it's not my fault. But I wonder whether she got the idea and then went looking for something to use, or whether she was just digging through magazines and stumbled across it and decided today was a fine day.

For the first time I look forward to Monday. I want to get away from the bruised and battered. I want to see someone, anyone, even for an instant, with happiness in her eyes. The smile of a child would be wonderful to look at. I'd like to sit down in a big soft chair and pat a dog.

In a few days, early in the morning, while everyone else is still asleep, I will be shackled and taken from this place under guard. I cannot imagine what it will feel like out there in the world again, trammeled though I'll be. This place, this madhouse, has become daily, ordinary, normal. And these women, a few of them, have become my friends. But I am eager, now, to leave them. Who knows what any one of them will do next? I care for Nina. But I think I'll be happy to get away from her.

And I am torn, at the same time, about leaving them all in such a time-out-of-mind place, under the huge flat thumb of mindless Madame Justice. They make a valiant attempt, the authorities, always to impose order, to structure our existence around rules and regulations, to make sense of us. But no matter how much order they summon or how stringently they apply it, it is artificial and therefore fraudulent, unsuccessful. The captors, they are the ones in prison. We prisoners can fall no farther, and because of that we are completely free. I don't know what I will do if I get back to the real world.

It is conceivable that after next week I won't return to this place. That's what I tell myself I want. To be found competent and go to trial, prove to everyone else, as a way of proving to myself, that I am not a murderer.

Dr. Hoffman has been his usual sly self. He has not given me so much as a hint about what his report contains, what he will testify to or what he thinks about my case. In some respects, he is the consummate shrink.

An opening door startles me, and there is the doctor himself, his head pulled back and up in a gesture of interrogation and surprise. What am I doing in Emma's room. Why am I not where I belong.

"I thought I left something here when you moved me," I explain. "And I was worried about Emma, after what Nina did. I wanted to see that she was all right."

"You have no business here," he tells me.

"I've been trying to convince you of that from the start," I say, stuffing the magazines back into the locker.

"Cynthia," he says, businesslike, "not tonight. Get back to your room where you belong."

"What will you tell them? I mean, it can't hurt to tell me now. What did you decide?"

He looks at me carefully, studying my face. I am concerned for a moment that something is wrong with me and he can see it there.

"Let's go to my office," he says. "Let's go and have a chat."

I'm startled. Amazed. Intrigued.

I wonder why he is wandering around the unit in the middle of the night. I follow Dr. Hoffman into the stairwell and down the hall to his office.

He turns on the single halogen lamp that sits in the center of his desk. The light it sends into the room seems extraordinarily white and makes sharp, detailed shadows. It is hard light, as unforgiving as time. It is how I feel being in this room with Dr. Hoffman. Everything in this place is hard and sharp. It is hours since "Lights out" was yelled down the hall by the hacks. They will come around to count us again at two o'clock. They'll go crazy if I am not in my bed. I wonder who this man is and what I am doing here. I wonder if Kissy will come looking for me. I wonder if she'll be all right until I get back to the room.

Tonight he does not in the least resemble my father. What shows on his face is overwork. Dismay. I think I see pity there, too. Yes, that's it, even as he's looking at me.

"Dr. Hoffman," I say, "please don't feel sorry for me."

"You don't belong here," he replies.

"I know that."

"You never should have been sent here in the first place."

"I know that, too."

"Why did you kill him?"

I don't know whether he is my friend. He seems to have called a truce. Maybe he just wants to know.

Maybe. I mustn't let my guard down. He may be trying to trap me. Like Kissy.

"I guess I married a man just like dear old Dad," I say. "Do you think that could be the problem?" Immediately I regret my sarcasm. Dr. Hoffman is up in the middle of the night, trying to talk to me, trying to listen.

Trying to help me?

I cannot trust him. I cannot. He has too much power over me and everyone else in this unit. Too much power, and power flourishes at the expense of love.

"I don't think you've ever mentioned him before."

"Mentioned who?"

"Your father, Cynthia. You've never so much as uttered a peep about him. What was he like?"

"I don't know."

"Surely you have some idea."

"I do not have a single idea of what he was like. I do not even have an impression."

"What do you remember of him."

"I try not to."

"Try."

"I would prefer not to."

"Wouldn't we all."

"All right then. Here is my impression of my father. My father always ate the food my mother put in front of him. Everyone had to be quiet when he was in the house. And my father hit my mother."

"And you?"

"I was not part of the equation. I simply stayed out of the way. As much as possible."

"Did he ever hit you?"

"No. He hit my sister once."

"You've never mentioned her, either."

"We were all at dinner together, which was itself unusual. My sister spilled her milk."

"And that's why he hit her?"

"I don't know why he hit her. That's when he hit her, after she spilled her milk. He knocked her out of her chair. Have you ever been around it, Dr. Hoffman?"

"Around?"

"Around, up close, when that kind of violence happens. When someone big and strong hauls off and whacks someone. Especially when it's someone who's small. Have you ever heard that sound?"

"Thankfully I haven't."

"Well, you don't hear it with your ears. You hear it in your bones. You hear it in your stomach. In your entire gut. And you never forget it. No matter how hard you try."

"Your father, was he . . . Did he do this sort of thing often?"

"She stayed out of school for the rest of the week because of the bruise. My mother kept her home. There was no way to hide it. On her cheek. Her left cheekbone. My sister was beautiful, doctor. She was stunning. And she knew how to love people, how to care about them. She was genuine. It's count time soon, I think. Perhaps I should go back to my room."

"Did you get along with your sister?"

"You see," I say, "he comes to me two ways. He comes as a dog. Not while I'm sleeping. It's not a nightmare. I can be wide awake, walking around, eating breakfast or whatever. Working on the mailbags. He comes as a dog. Vicious. Snarling. From behind stairways or out of closets or from beneath the bed. Or maybe I'll be walking in a park and he comes from behind a bush. Going for my throat."

"And in this fantasy," the doctor says, "what happens? Does the dog bite you? Does it kill you?"

"No. I mean I don't know. It's never killed me — that I know of. I always manage to get hold of it. To try to stop it. But I never make it to the end of the story. Something always happens to snap me out of it before I find out what happens. It is coming at me and I am struggling to get hold of it to stop it, but I never get to the end. It's getting worse. It's making me feel faint when it happens. It's making me feel as though I might . . ."

"Might?"

I cannot tell him that I am afraid I will snap out of it and find I have hurt someone. Someone who just happens to bump into me on the street. I cannot tell him that.

"Nothing," I say. "It just scares me, the way it makes me feel."

"That's perfectly normal," he says. "I'd only be concerned if it didn't frighten you."

"Dr. Hoffman," I say, "I got along with her wonderfully. I mean, we were very different, but I loved her, and I'm sure she loved me. We weren't the closest, you know, but we were sisters. I can forgive him for what he did to me. But I cannot forgive him for what he did to her."

He sits for a long time, looking at nothing.

"You've thought about this a great deal," he says finally. More silence. Too much silence.

"The other way he comes is as a stranger. When there is noise so that I can't hear his approach. He sneaks up behind, with something awful in his hand. Some kind of weapon."

"And?"

"So far I've always managed to stop the noise before he makes it close enough to reach me."

He folds his hands in front of his mouth and closes his eyes. He looks as though he is praying.

This is neither the time nor the place, in this sterile office in the middle of the night with a man I do not know, but they come flooding. The pain pours from my eyes and runs down my face. So huge is what I feel that there are not separate, distinct tears, but tears building one upon the next so quickly that rivulets of water stream from my burning eyes. I hear myself choking, sobbing, gasping, and I am crying for her death, for her short time, for who she was and who she could have become had I not brought Daniel into our lives. I am crying because I know I will never understand why I wasn't enough, why he had to go after her, too. I am trying to understand what drove me to kill him and save myself. I am understanding what it means to have taken a human life. He will be with me for as long as I live. Part of me. I will carry him inside. Instead of his child in my womb, I have him, clinging to my spine, right between my shoulderblades, ready to reach out and squeeze my heart dry if I give him the slightest opening. If I cry hard enough, long enough, maybe I can wash him out of me. Where is this coming from? Foolish me. I hear John Lennon in my head: *Cry, baby, cry. Make your mother sigh. You're old enough to know better . . .*

"Cynthia," Dr. Hoffman says, and crosses his legs. He speaks gently, quietly. I calm myself. There are tears now. Clear, silent drops of regret, slipping from the corners of my eyes. "You don't have to forgive him for what he did to someone else, even someone you loved dearly. In fact, you're exactly right. You can't forgive him for that. What was between them was between them. It wasn't up to you. Only she could have forgiven him for what he did to her."

"But she never would have met him if I hadn't. I brought him into her life. She would still be alive."

"No, Cynthia. Their paths crossed. Your sister made her choices, her decisions. Maybe she saw what he was about, maybe she didn't. We can't know. If it hadn't been Daniel, it might well have been someone else. There are hundreds of subtle cues that people react to when they meet each other, when they see each other. Perhaps on some level she understood that this was an abusive man, that he would hurt her. And perhaps she thought she deserved that kind of treatment. That may have been what intrigued her. What led her to get involved with him."

"Are you telling me that my sister walked into Daniel's life with a sign on her forehead that said Hit Me and he responded to that? He liked that?"

"That's one way of looking at it. There was something about this man that attracted your sister. Maybe it was his abusiveness. It happens every day. You are not responsible for her choices or his. You have to let that part of it go. Let it go."

I know what he is going to say before he says it.

About the other part. About me.

I am stunned to think it, yet I probably have known it for some time now. The dynamic he has described between my sister and Daniel is the same one that operated for me.

And it is the same one that operated between my parents. And, though I am not certain, I suspect it was there between each of their parents as well.

"You cannot forgive him for what he did to her. But you can forgive her for what she did to you."

He is right. She is the one I must forgive. She took herself away from this world. Away from people who loved her. Away from me and from our mother.

"Do you know why you're crying?" he asks gently.

"For lots of reasons," I stutter. "I guess it just all built up."

"You are mourning the loss of your victimization," he says.

"Dr. Hoffman," I say, "how does one break the chain? How does one undo all those years?"

He hands me a tissue, and then, smiling kindly, pulls three more from the box and holds them out to me.

"One afternoon," he says, "Carl Jung was walking down the street. He bumped into his uncle, who said, 'Do you know how the devil tortures souls in hell?' Jung thought for a long moment. Finally his uncle looked at him, raised a single finger and said, 'He keeps them waiting.'

"Cynthia," he adds, "all men are not like your father. I think you've been waiting quite long enough."

.   .   .

I wander down the white-bright hallways, past darkened rooms holding sleeping inmates. Past Harold snoozing on the orange couch. The voice of David Letterman cuts into the television blue shadows of the dayroom. I am comforted, I think, to know the world is still out there, laughing.

Light from the hallway slices across the floor of 310 when I open the door, disappears quickly as I close it.

Kissy sits on her bed, her feet propped on the mattress rail, arms flopped across her knees. She raises her head as I enter.

"How could you do that?" she says. "How could you just walk out on me when I was trying to tell you something really important?"

"I'm sorry, Kissy. It was urgent."

"What was so urgent? Why were you gone such a long time? Where have you been? You've been crying."

"One, I can't tell you. Two, I ran into Dr. Hoffman. Three, in his office. Four, yes."

"Oh," she says, and then begins laughing softly to herself. She shakes her head and says, "Tell you what, sweetheart: you wash, I'll dry."

"Do you want to finish what you were telling me? I really am sorry, Kissy. I know it was important. What were you saying?"

"What was Hoffman doing in the unit at this hour?"

"I don't know. But we had a good talk."

"I find that hard to believe."

"He's not so awful. I've even begun to think that he has a good heart. God only knows why he works in a place like this."

"God and the Department of Justice." She flops back on her bed. "So I guess I was in the middle of trying to kill myself when you suddenly had to leave. Is that where we were?"

"Something like that, yes."

"Well, I thought about it while you were gone and decided I didn't really want to kill myself. It was just like I said. I had to let the pressure out."

"It's understandable," I say. "Though somewhat drastic."

"I hadn't yet discovered aerobics." She smiles. "Ha."

"Are things better now?"

"Now?" she says. "Now? Cynthia, now I'm in jail. No, things aren't better. Wait a minute. That's not true."

"Kissy," I say, "nothing you've said since the day I met you is true. Why start telling the truth now?"

"You're exactly right. No. Wait a minute. You want the truth, sweetheart? I'll give you the truth. Whole and nothing but. We have some things in common."

I can't believe she's going to come clean.

"I was never a professor of English," she says. "I never got popped for fabric subversion or immigration violations or anything else like that. I don't have a niece. I don't have a sister. I have one brother who lives on Staten Island and makes lamps out of leftover pieces of metal and signs them Bad Bob on the base and makes a fortune selling them in little SoHo furniture boutiques. We haven't spoken for years. Wanna know why?"

I nod.

"Because he hated, absolutely despised, my lover. From the start he hated her. For six years he hated her. He told me she was trouble and that it would end in disaster. Know what?"

"She?" I ask. "I thought you said you slept with your shrink. And he was a he."

She sits up and leans forward in the dark.

"Yes, she. Cynthia, what planet are you on? In case you hadn't noticed, I go both ways. No big deal. I'm not after your bod. But if you ever decide . . ." She tosses her head and laughs, and I join her, laughing at my own shortsightedness, relieved to be laughing after what happened in the doctor's office. Then suddenly she is serious again. "Anyway," she says, "my brother was absolutely right. It ended in disaster. It ended in me doing exactly the same thing you did, even though you won't admit it. Only I used a car, sweetheart. Even though we were never officially married, you know, we had exchanged vows. And for a long time I believed in us. We were going to buy some sperm and have a child. But things got so bad. So bad. She lost herself completely, turned into one of these macho bitches who are always trying to prove how manly they are. Till death do us part? I speeded things up a bit, honey bunch. Do you know why? Because I was tired of getting the shit beat outta me every single goddam night by this meshuga motherfucker. I swear to you, as long as I live I will cherish the memory of the look on her face. No, wait, wait. Listen. When she saw me behind the wheel and realized, at that last instant, that there was no way I could stop, and then realized that there was no way I was even going to *try* to stop? Priceless."

This woman is mad. Madder than Nina, mad in a dangerous way.

"Elizabeth," I say, "shall we try to get some sleep?"

I lie back and take off my watch and fold my hand around it. It strikes me that Kissy — or Elizabeth or whoever she is — is no different from her lover. No different from Daniel. The relationship wasn't about love. It was only about who would have the upper hand. I can feel it here in the room.

Kissy had murder in her heart long before she ever met her girlfriend. The very thing she despised in her lover — the drive for power — was what she despised in herself. The relationship was only an excuse.

I fought back once. I knew the effort was foolish, that he would overpower me and perhaps strike harder because I'd dared to try. But it happened before I could restrain myself. It happened in a ditch on the side of a highway.

I was driving; I was fleeing. Escaping forever. I had to try. I had to see whether it was only bluster, whether he would cower if I stood up to him. I had to know whether I could get him to leave me alone, to let me live my life without the terror he'd brought into it. I think I knew the answer before I made the effort. But I had to give him the chance to go away.

He pulled his car up next to mine, so close, mere inches away, and he was halfway across the front seat, his left hand on the wheel and his right one slamming the back of the seat as he screamed, raged at me to pull over. I gripped the wheel and drove, accelerating, pressing the gas pedal to the floor. There was only the dark blur through which I drove, a three A.M. tunnel with destruction at either end. It was dreamlike: I saw myself clinging to the steering wheel of a convertible, my body flapping in the breeze like an old sheet. I gripped hard. I tried to steer, but the car was going where it would; I had nothing to do with it.

Daniel slammed me once, and again, and the second time sent my car into the ditch. I felt my face hit the wheel, mud beneath the car, tons of metal sliding helplessly down into the ditch while I held on, single green blades of grass passing in slow motion, glowing in the March moonlight, and all I could see then was the face of my sister, the face of my sister, Alice, and she'd been dead for less than a month and I knew even then he'd forced her to it.

When the car stopped I looked in the sideview mirror and watched numbly as Daniel climbed from his car and staggered toward me.

The occasional vehicle screamed past in the night while he explained to me that I should be a good wife. I told myself that the drivers flying by must not be able to see what was going on, what he was doing to convince me to come home and love him.

12 "You will meet someone," Herlinda says, "and you will know he is good, he is the right one, and you will marry him and have four children." Her face hovers beside the mayonnaise jar full of water. Next to it burn two candles. Louisa sits close to her, smiling and looking from the water to me and back again, trying to understand what Herlinda is telling me. Lulu stands at the door of the workroom.

"Three boys and a girl. Gringita," Herlinda says, "you

will be happy. It will not be like the last time. You will be happy."

"How do you know these things, Herlinda? How can you tell me I'll be happy?"

She leans back from the jar, begins playing with one of her necklaces.

"I see it in the water." She smiles. "And he is a handsome man, too. And very, very smart."

"I wish I could believe it," I tell her.

"It is not only what I see in the water," she says quietly. "So many people think happiness is this magical state that descends upon you. They say they are always looking for it but can't find it. But happiness isn't out there hiding, waiting to be found. And it doesn't fall from the sky and land on your head. It is something you decide. You decide to make choices that will make you happy. Does that make sense to you?"

"I think so."

"Look at it this way," she says. "You know the commandments, the one that goes love thy neighbor as thyself?"

"Yes," I say, "of course I know it. But I've been trying not to think too much about that lately."

"Well, think about this. Do you love yourself when you act badly toward someone else? When you lie to them or mistreat them? No. I don't think so. You don't even *like* yourself when you hurt other people. So if you are supposed to love your neighbor as yourself, then you won't love them when they lie to you. You won't love them if they hit you. Not even God would demand that of you. If you want happiness, make choices that let you be happy. And be with people who also know to make those decisions."

Lulu leans out the door and then scurries to her stool and grabs a mailbag.

"Svejk," she says.

Louisa hides the jar and candles behind a pile of rejected mailbags in a corner of the room and is just sitting down when Svejk walks in.

"Today's luncheon menu, ladies," he drawls. "We have beef porcupines, green beans, rice, rolls and pudding."

I do not even lift the plastic cover off the plastic plate on which rests my portion of beef porcupine. I do not know what it is, cannot imagine it, and do not want to find out. I take a roll and a glass of Kool-Aid. Herlinda stands next to me and removes her tray from the cart.

"Just remember, gringita," she says. "It is up to you to save your own soul. Nobody else's."

I take my roll and Kool-Aid and go to my room.

Glenda is down in the courtyard, but instead of dancing she is striking poses, holding each one for several minutes. She looks, at the moment, like an art deco lamp figurine, standing on her toes with her back arched and her arms folded across her chest. I do not know how she manages to balance, but she stays that way for some time before going limp and crumpling to the ground, balled up, her long dark hair splayed over the green concrete. I cannot imagine her reality, what kind of world she lives in. I only know that in spite of her claims of complete and total goodness within, there is something sad and awful in her smile. Something hunted in her smile. She is not connected. She exists in a world apart, far away from the rest of us. I don't know what it is that has chased her to that place, but it must be terribly lonely out there.

·   ·   ·

I stand next to Kissy at our door. I see Emma across the hall. Janna's fingers wiggle through the wire mesh in the doorway next to mine.

"Fuck count time," she says, "and all you bitches with it. Think anyone gives a rat's ass about who you are or what you do? These hacks, they get an order to take us all out and line us up and shoot us, they'll do it, bitches. They'll do whatever they're told to do. Better believe it. Better believe it! They'da made great Nazis, but not a one of 'em could cut it as a hijacker. They wouldn't know how to rob a bank if they took lessons from John Dillinger."

She goes on. The hack comes down the hall. Today is mail day. Dear Dad (I would have written), I don't know why you had such a life. I don't know why you tormented yourself and your family. I wish we could have loved each other more openly. (Because I know, Dad, that you loved me and I loved you.) I wish you could have learned not to hate yourself. Then you could have let your family love you. You could have learned not to sabotage things. Your daughter, Cynthia.

I could never have mailed it. Inmates open their letters as they turn back through doorways and into their rooms. Kissy has three, and goes immediately to her bed and rips one open. I sit watching her read. The letter takes her elsewhere, brings a smile to her face. She is completely unaware of me. I saw him like that once. I was to meet Daniel at a jeweler's in Dallas where we would order our wedding rings. He wanted them custom-made; he wanted them to be unique. I got there a few minutes early and took the elevator to the eleventh floor. I was waiting in the anteroom when I saw the elevator door open and there he was, lost in thought, unaware for just that instant that the door had opened. He thought he was standing alone and unseen inside the wood-paneled, carpeted box, and in that moment I saw him as he saw himself: confused and a little frightened, hoping that he was making the right decision, that he wasn't rushing into things, hoping that he could be the kind of husband and father he said he would be. It was only for the shortest bit of time that I saw him that way, only a second or two before he realized the elevator was open and saw me and put on his game face. I was so touched by this glimpse of vulnerability that I wanted to take him in my arms and rock him like a baby, comfort him and tell him everything would be all right. But I knew he could never admit feeling that way.

I am embarrassed, now, watching Kissy while she reads. I feel like a voyeur. I lie down and turn my face to the wall and wait for the hack to announce count clear. Washington, hence America, will rest easy, knowing that we are all in our places. I don't know where I will go when I get out of this place.

I don't know if I'll get out of this place.

13

The courtroom is intimate, with only five or six short rows of churchlike pews holding the scattered spectators who've come for whatever reason. I recognize none of them. But there is Dr. Hoffman, talking to the prosecutor, a mask of professionalism hiding his everyday face. I think of last night, doubt whether I should have talked to him. I picture him wearing one of Kissy's green facial masks to stop myself from second-guessing.

The furniture here is modern, not unlike that of the day-room, but made of wood instead of Formica. There is dark blue carpeting, wall to government wall. There is the Great Seal of the United States behind the judge's bench, and all the men in this room are white and wear suits, except for one dark-skinned man in a brown uniform who stands near the door through which, I suppose, the judge will enter.

I've seen this sort of thing before, on the evening or late night news: brief glimpses, artists' renderings of people standing before judges, being sentenced, or live footage of people walking out through courtroom doors and down slick marble halls. The news programs always had about them an air of unreality, of being just another television program.

Now I can look around and see that this is indeed a real place, holding real people. I can't change the channel and make the actors disappear. I wonder how many people have done this, have passed through this room to whatever fate a judge or jury handed them. I wonder what kind of person chooses to be a judge, seeks that office, that kind of power. Perhaps for many it is merely another career path, something attorneys follow without giving it a great deal of thought.

With jurors it's different; they've been called, forced to appear, do their duty. They come and sit in the box and watch from a civic distance as the lawyers hurl words at each other.

Sitting here at the defense table, I have a sudden vision of the judge rolling through the door into the courtroom, not in the traditional black robes, but in the black and white stripes of a basketball referee, waving his arms and blowing a metal whistle. That might add a sporting joviality to the juridical *mise en scène,* far truer to what is happening here than the pomp and circumstance that are the order of the day.

Perhaps Dr. Hoffman would be right if he labels me incompetent.

The bailiff draws himself to full height and shouts, "All rise," but I do not listen to the rest of what he says. I feel blood draining from my head, pooling in my feet; my head is filled with heavy emptiness. I close my eyes. I want to sleep. The bailiff's voice bangs through my ears to the inside, bouncing off the bones of my skull. The United States of America versus Cynthia Mitchell. A hand on my arm, firmly, urges me to stand. My lawyer. We are in the arena. Or is it a theater?

I wish I knew her better.

"Look at the judge," she reminds me in a whisper. "Make eye contact."

I do as she says, but the Honorable Melvin D. Wulf, looking pasty-faced and hung over, and bored on top of it, is arranging his robes to sit down.

"Be seated," he says, and I try not to look as if I am collapsing as I sit. My legs are down there somewhere. I close my eyes.

Judge Wulf says something. The prosecutor says something. My lawyer says something. I sit listening to their voices, their word volleys. I can hear tones, modulations, the rising and falling of sentences. Where are their words?

The judge sounds angry. I look at the empty jury box and for a moment see ghosts from past trials sitting there in the padded chairs.

Now the prosecutor again. His name is Marchander and his voice is beige and shuddery.

"Dr. Hoffman, Your Honor."

The judge thanks him. Dr. Hoffman swears to tell the whole truth and sits down in the witness stand.

"Has the court been provided with a copy of Exhibit A, Dr. Hoffman's report, and Exhibit B, Dr. Hoffman's curriculum vitae, which goes on for twenty-six pages? I would invite the court's attention to these exhibits and move to Dr. Hoffman's testimony, unless there's some objection from the court or the defense?"

My lawyer does not object. Judge Wulf nods his approval and says, "Proceed."

Mr. Marchander faces the witness.

"Dr. Hoffman," he says, "you have had in your custody and under your observation for these past ten weeks a Ms. Cynthia Mitchell. Correct?"

"In my capacity as the chief psychiatrist at the Veritas Unit of the Fort Worth Federal Correctional Institution, yes, I have."

"And you have administered various psychological tests and physical examinations to Ms. Mitchell over the course of those ten weeks?"

"Yes, sir."

"Now, based on those tests and examinations, and on your general observations of Ms. Mitchell, as well as the tests and examinations you have administered, do you have an opinion within a reasonable degree of scientific certainty as to Ms. Mitchell's competency to stand trial?"

"Well, I had to do considerable analysis of what staff members observed, and what other people said about her at her bail hearing, when she was originally given over to my custody for observation, to see whether it fit what I was seeing."

"And did it?"

"Well, for a period of time, approximately six weeks into her stay with us, Ms. Mitchell had to be detained in the high-security wing because she had begun exhibiting symptoms similar to those which had been described to me as occurring during her bail hearing."

The judge leans forward and waves Mr. Marchander back.

"What did you observe," the judge says, "that led you to place the defendant in high security?"

"I'm not going to pretend that this is not a complicated case, Your Honor. Ms. Mitchell appeared to be experiencing a psychosis. I observed a marked loosening of associations in addition to delusions, hallucinations and severely disorganized behavior."

The judge does not look pleased. I wonder why Dr. Hoffman doesn't tell them that I was fine until he put me in that room and began torturing me. I could tell the judge about the numbness. I could tell how it wasn't psychosis at all; it was only Daniel haunting me.

"Speak in layman's terms, please, doctor," the judge says.

"In layman's terms, Your Honor, Ms. Mitchell experienced a brief reactive psychosis."

"English, please, doctor."

"She was attempting to cope with a horrible trauma, and in doing so she went a little crazy for a brief period of time."

"Has she recovered? In your opinion?"

"In my estimation, yes, she has."

"Very well. Mr. Marchander, will you please ask the good doctor your question once again?"

"Based on your general observations of Ms. Mitchell, as well as the various tests and examinations you have administered, do you have an opinion within a reasonable degree of scientific certainty as to Ms. Mitchell's competency to stand trial?"

"I do."

"And what is that opinion?"

"That she is competent to stand trial."

"Is she capable of understanding the charges against her and of assisting in her defense?"

"I believe she is."

Mr. Marchander looks smugly at the judge, who responds by turning to stare at me. My lawyer has no questions.

"And as for the defendant," Judge Wulf says, "has she anything to add to this morning's proceedings?"

"Nothing, Your Honor," says my lawyer. I feel invisible.

"Well then, ladies and gentlemen," the judge says, "I'm sure the magistrate who saw Ms. Mitchell at her bail hearing felt it necessary to place the defendant in custody for evaluation because of what he described as her bizarre behavior. But I'm satisfied that we may proceed. I'm going to call a recess for lunch until one o'clock this afternoon, at which time we will choose a jury and hear opening remarks from the government."

At lunch, Debra tells me I should eat something.

"Be calm," she says. "We're ready for them."

Though she has prepared me for the questions, I don't feel ready.

By midafternoon, the jury is chosen. I wonder what they think, sitting there waiting to hear the details. They do not resemble any peers I've known. Two of them remind me of Daniel. One because he resembles him physically — the dark hair, the sharp blue eyes, the outdoor complexion. And he's obviously athletic, though I haven't seen him move a muscle since he was seated. The other doesn't so much look like Daniel as seem like him. Something in his razor-straight posture belies anger contained.

I wouldn't have seen that before. I would have mistaken his demeanor the way I mistook Daniel's. It wasn't until after we were married that I recognized the extent of his rage; I thought until then that his occasional impatience was provoked because he was keen and full of integrity, because he had trouble dealing with incompetence. But isn't that the phrase: it wasn't until after we were married . . . Perhaps all the hope and anticipation clouds one's vision, and it is only well after "I do" that the haze drifts away.

I wonder whether I'll be required, forced, to tell these strangers in the jury box that I was a fool. Will I admit that I possessed powers of denial heretofore unseen in the Western world? I wanted Daniel to be a kind and loving husband. Therefore he was. Regardless of how often he hit me.

I thought then that surely there must be a reason. I thought I must have been doing something to deserve it.

"The first count," Mr. Marchander says, "the Grand Jury, by this indictment, accuse the defendant, Cynthia Mitchell, of the crime of murder, committed as follows.

"The defendant, Cynthia Mitchell, on or about April 10, 1988, with intent to cause the death of a person, did cause the death of one Daniel Mitchell by stabbing him repeatedly with a knife.

"Ladies and gentlemen, this is the crime with which the defendant is charged."

He stops and takes a long look at me. I return his stare and then look past him at the jury. Their faces are blank. They are not even here. I do not know whether my feeling toward the prosecutor is hatred or fear.

"What the evidence will show" — Marchander slaps a hand

gently on the wooden front of the jury box — "it will show that Cynthia Stratton, a college-educated young woman who worked in public relations, met, fell in love with and, in September of 1986, married Daniel Mitchell, a commercial airline pilot. It will show that soon after the marriage, Daniel's behavior began to change. Instead of being a loving husband who was looking forward to having a family, Daniel became abusive, not only psychologically and emotionally, but often physically. The evidence will show that Cynthia Mitchell, instead of trying to escape from this abuse, continued to live with Daniel as his wife, did nothing to get him any kind of help, sought no treatment for herself, her husband or for the two of them as a married couple. And the evidence will show that Cynthia Mitchell, who, ladies and gentlemen, may try to tell you that she was only defending herself against her husband, was not in fact protecting herself from anything or anyone when she stabbed her husband to death. What the evidence will show, ladies and gentlemen, is that Cynthia Mitchell murdered Daniel Mitchell in cold blood as he lay sleeping in their tent while the two of them were on a camping trip. And that after brutally murdering Daniel, she dug a hole in the ground and placed his body in it, and then packed up their bloodstained camping gear and returned to what had been their home, ladies and gentlemen. Went on for five entire days as though nothing had happened."

He stands there for a moment, letting his words melt over the jury like so much wax.

"And would have continued to do so, would have erased this man's memory from the face of the earth without a trace, without a sign, without so much as a tear of remorse, had not Daniel's friends at work become alarmed by his failure to return from vacation."

I sit watching the prosecutor, watching his performance.

He could not begin to know what went on. He walks back and forth slowly, in front of the jury, calling me calculating, calling me cold-blooded, calling me a murderer.

Suddenly I see myself getting up from the defense table, walking over to where he is, planting myself squarely in front of him and bursting into song: *Call me irresponsible, call me unreliable . . .*

It is all so irrelevant. My being here is irrelevant. I am but the latest in a never-ending line of defendants. More will come after me. This little ferret will keep drawing up the papers and putting on the prosecutions and getting people locked up, locked away, put out of sight, maybe even get some of us executed, but it has nothing to do with reality. It does nothing to change the hows and whys.

He is walking over to sit down now. He is finished with his opening statement.

My lawyer stands.

I hear words coming out of her mouth, but they aren't hers. They are Daniel's. I remembered them too well. I remembered them verbatim. I quoted them. I told her what he said that last night in the tent. So calm, he was. He lay there next to me and he could have been talking about a future full of love. His tone was like that.

"Don't ever try to leave me," he said. "Don't ever try to go anyplace. I'll kill you. You know, don't you, Cynthia," he said, "that I'm telling you the truth?"

I hear his words coming out of my lawyer's mouth.

" 'If you try to run,' " she says, " 'I'll start with your mother. No, I'll start with your sister's dogs. Your mother has them now, doesn't she? Now that poor Alice has killed herself? God, I miss her. First the dogs. And then I'll get your mother.'

"He threatened to kill them one by one," she says.

"Ladies and gentlemen," she says, "he told Cynthia that if she ever tried to leave, he would kill her mother and then he would kill her."

Those are the words.

"Frightened out of her mind," my lawyer says. "Knowing that going to the police or the courts to get a piece of paper to try to stop this man was to court not just her own death, but possibly that of her mother as well . . ."

I look at the people in the jury box; they are looking at my lawyer. One woman glances at me, for an instant, but I see in her eyes that she knows firsthand what is being spoken of here.

"The only way to stop him," my lawyer says, "the only way to end the beatings — being thrown against the wall, being kicked and clubbed — was to be quiet. To be the passive wife that Daniel Mitchell valued above everything, above even life itself. Cynthia Mitchell knew what this man was capable of. She knew what he had done and what he threatened to do if she tried to escape the living hell that he had created for the both of them."

I sit and listen as my lawyer says, "Confused." "Bewildered," she says. "In despair," she says. Those words do not convey it. There are no words to tell what was happening. These actors, posturing about the room, lawyers and judges trying to deconstruct reality, adapt it to their own vision of what the world should be — what do they know of terror? Everyone here is dressed nicely, hair combed and in place, the men's ties neatly knotted, the women appropriately made up, their real and various faces hidden beneath varying masks of paint. *Confused,* my lawyer said. *Bewildered,* my lawyer said. *In despair,* my lawyer said.

What my lawyer cannot convey, what I cannot convey, what the jury and judge and prosecutor can never understand, is how small it was. How small and squalid. How quick and measly it was. How dirty.

It was.

The ropelike muscles in his forearm pressing my face to the dirt, the smell of fear in his sweat, glistening, glaring, the trees cowering silently above, the night sky ink-blue, pimpled with stars gloating silently in their heaven at my awful nakedness. His skin against mine, the taut raging weight of his anger pressing me, his spine arched against the night, pushing me into the dirt, pushing my face into the dirt, *from dust you came, bitch.*

He howled his love song into the silence of the long deep forest. He filled me up with his love. He dragged me, broken and bleeding, back into the tent.

"Never leave me," he whispered. "Try to leave me and you'll die."

I remember being thirsty. Terribly, terribly thirsty.

"The government calls Elliot Donatich to the stand."

I've never seen this man who is sitting in the witness box and sneaking looks at me, glancing his horror in my direction. He has gone pale.

"State your name," the prosecutor says.

He does, and the prosecutor asks him to spell it.

"Mr. Donatich, will you tell your age, please."

"Thirty-seven."

"Married or single?"

"Married."

"Employed?"

"Yes."

"And what sort of work do you do?"

"I'm an accountant."

"Mr. Donatich, let me direct your attention to April 15, 1988, approximately eleven o'clock in the morning. Do you recall where you were at that time, sir?"

"Yes, I do. I was hiking in the Big Thicket, along a seldom-used trail."

"Would that be the Big Thicket National Preserve, located just north of Kountze?"

"Yes, sir, that's the one. I camp there frequently."

"That's kind of a swampy forest, isn't it?"

"Yes, sir."

"And while you were hiking, did you have occasion to notice anything unusual?"

"I did. Actually my dog did, or . . ."

"Tell us, Mr. Donatich, in your own words, what happened to you that morning. What you discovered, or what happened with your dog. Just tell us what happened."

"I was hiking. My dog was running through the forest along with me, you know, sometimes on the trail, sometimes leaving it for a few minutes to explore in the woods. He left the trail for what seemed to me a pretty long time. I stopped, and started calling him, whistling for him. He's real well trained and obedient, but he didn't return."

"Go on."

"I left the trail and went into the woods to look for him. I found him pawing at a mound of dirt not too far off the trail."

"And what did you do?"

"I leashed him and hiked back to the ranger's shack to report what I'd found."

"And what was it exactly, Mr. Donatich, that you'd found?"

"A man's body."

"Thank you, Mr. Donatich."

He calls someone else, and I recognize the agent who came to the house and arrested me and took me to where Daniel's body had been found. His face showed shock when I first opened the door. My own face was still a mess; I hadn't bothered to try to cover any of the bruises with make-up.

The agent's partner had a camera with him, and he took Polaroids of me as soon as the handcuffs were on. I felt deep shame as the flash went off in my eyes, but I understood that they had to protect themselves against charges of brutality. Later, at the jail, when I was stripped and searched, the matron had more photos taken, of my arms and legs and back.

Now the agent is on the stand, saying I offered no resistance, no alibi and no explanation. I had none.

Each and every member of the jury is looking at me as if I am a hideous apparition, something that has just crawled out of the depths of hell and slithered into this chair at the defense table. I am an abomination. I am less than human.

Mr. Marchander finishes with him, short and sweet, passes the witness. My lawyer tells Judge Wulf that she wishes to reserve the right to call the agent later, when the defense presents its case. She has no questions at the moment.

She wasn't there. I don't know how long I lay in the tent. I listened from far away as Daniel's breathing settled, as he drifted from consciousness into sleep. I touched my cheek, near my right eye where it felt swollen, and my fingers came away bloody. I wondered why I couldn't feel pain, and then I remembered that it never came until much later, when I was alone and it was safe to feel again.

I lay there next to him and thought about sneaking out of the tent and running. That was all I could think of for the longest time. About escape.

And then I understood that as long as he was alive there would be no escape. There would be no reprieve from his violence. As long as he was alive, I would be beaten. As long as he was alive, I would live in terror for myself and for those I loved. And soon, perhaps even tonight, he would kill me. Maybe it would be an accident. It wouldn't matter. As long as he was alive, he would be trying to kill me.

I did not hate him so much for that; I understood that I could never know what was driving him to it, what was causing his pain, tormenting him. I hated him for holding a dream in front of my eyes and then shattering it while I watched. I hated him for having lured me into a snare he'd laid as cold-bloodedly as though he were a fur trapper. The hatred was so strong I almost felt it as a force going from my body to his as he lay sleeping there that night, and then it was as though it were simply draining out of me, the hatred, no longer directed at him, seeping through the tent bottom and into the earth below us.

I heard a small animal rustling in the woods and I crept out of the tent. His camping knife lay near the fire, which was now in dead gray embers. Morning felt close.

I looked long at the knife and tried to feel something. I saw myself from the edge of the clearing, saw a woman kneeling by the dead fire, holding a large knife, picking at the inside of her wrist with its glistening point. Small fluttery cuts, just barely deep enough to draw thin rivulets of blood. Testing to see if her body was real. Testing to see if she was there.

Then she stood up and moved silently toward the tent, still trying to feel something, and as she entered, she realized what it was that filled her, what had replaced all the hatred and fear that had drained away. She looked at the sleeping form on the floor of the tent and felt utter, complete and undiluted indifference.

". . . multiple stab wounds to the neck and chest," someone is saying. A white man in a dark suit on the witness stand has replaced the agent who took me from the house. He is a doctor. A medical examiner. The forensic expert. Now it is their turn. The body. The man who found it. The officers who arrested me. The forensic expert sits on the stand and doesn't look at me. He couldn't care less about any of this. Good for him. Later, when it is our turn, my lawyer will call our witnesses. More experts. My mother. Me. We will each take the stand and tell our own versions. But she cannot call Alice. Alice has already told her side of the story.

Mr. Marchander asks something.

"There were no indications that any kind of struggle went on," the examiner replies. "No defensive wounds of any kind."

"Defensive wounds?"

"Cuts to indicate that he was defending himself. If the subject were conscious and attempting to fend off an attack, he would normally have slashes to the hands or forearms from having raised them against his attacker. There was none of that with this subject."

Mr. Marchander passes the witness.

"Doctor," my lawyer says, rising, "does the lack of these so-called defensive wounds absolutely rule out the possibility that Mr. Mitchell might have been awake and actively defending himself?"

"No, it does not."

"And does it rule out the possibility that perhaps Mr. Mitchell was the one doing the attacking?"

"No, it does not."

"In other words, the fact that someone as big and strong as Mr. Mitchell was attacking Mrs. Mitchell might account for the lack of these wounds you're talking about."

"Well," he says, "yes, that's one possible scenario. But we . . ."

"Thank you, doctor," my lawyer says. "No further questions."

"We'll call it a day," the judge says. "Reconvene tomorrow morning at nine."

"Eye contact," my lawyer whispers.

I turn to look at the jury as they file out of the room.

"I'm going to urge you to speak up," Ms. Cohen says, "so that you can be heard by everyone." She looks sharp in her armor. Another dark suit, another silk bow, a different pair of well-polished, low-heeled pumps. Her nails are manicured, her hair tied neatly in place, her make-up impeccable. She is ready for battle.

"I'm going to ask you to tell the jury how old you are," she says.

"I'm thirty-three."

"And where were you born?"

"Fort Worth, Texas." These are easy. She is being gentle.

I tell of high school, college, the move to New York, the job, of meeting Daniel. These are easy but getting harder.

"And you gave up that job when Mr. Mitchell asked you to marry him and move back to Texas?"

"I did. I continued to do some freelance work after I moved, but I didn't go out and get a full-time position. There were offers. I just — Daniel and I planned to have children."

"Right after marriage?"

"Well, soon. Whenever it happened."

"After you were married, where did you and Daniel Mitchell live?"

"We lived in a house that he had before our wedding, north of Dallas, not far from DFW Airport."

"Did you love him?"

I'm not sure what she means. I don't know how to answer this. Did I love him? It was long ago. Not chronologically; otherwise. It was so long ago I can barely remember loving him. I can no longer be sure that I did. Perhaps because I cannot imagine living with the horror he created. I must have loved him. I was ready to bear his children. That is true love. That is love. I loved him. But I cannot imagine it now; I do not know how I could have. I don't remember what love feels like. I have forgotten how to feel anything.

"Yes," I say, but only because it is the answer she and I have agreed upon.

"How was the marriage, in the beginning?"

"It was fine. It was very, very good, but only for a few weeks. Then it changed."

"In what way?"

"He began beating me."

These words, they come out easily, as though I am saying, "He took up painting."

"A little louder, please," the judge says.

"Cynthia," Ms. Cohen says, "you'll have to speak up."

"He began beating me," I say loudly, and the sound system screeches feedback. I pull back from the microphone that hovers in front of my mouth, catching and amplifying every word. "I'm sorry," I say. "He began beating me." Still too loudly, as if announcing the magnitude of my foolishness.

"And this began only a few weeks into the marriage?"

"Yes. Two or three, I think."

"What did you do when this — what did you do the first time it happened?"

"I didn't do anything."

"Why not?"

"Because I was afraid. Because I thought it was a one-time thing. I thought some kind of pressure had gotten to him and he had just kind of flipped out. He swore to me it would never, ever happen again. He told me he loved me. He told me he wanted us to have a family. I believed him."

"And what about the second time?"

"I tried to leave. I tried to escape."

"And what happened?"

"He chased me down the freeway and ran my car off the road."

"Anything else?"

"That was the first time he told me that if I ever tried to leave he would kill me."

"And did you believe him then, too?"

"He gave me no reason not to."

"How many times, Cynthia, did your husband beat you? How often did this happen?"

"Not so frequently at first. Those first several months of our marriage, not more than two or three times."

"And later?"

"There wasn't any pattern to it. He would come home from a flight and, without any warning, push me up against the wall, begin slapping me, accusing me of having slept with his friends."

"Did you?"

"Absolutely not."

"Never?"

"Never."

"But there was no way to convince your husband of that."

"None. I learned better than to try. It only made him angrier, more violent."

"How big was your husband?"

"He was just over six feet tall. He was not a small man."

"And in good shape, physically?"

"Yes. He lifted weights regularly. He was a very strong, very athletic man."

"There wasn't much chance of your overpowering him?"

"Objection, Your Honor. Form." Mr. Marchander waits until he catches Ms. Cohen's eye before smiling.

"Sustained."

"Did you ever fight back? Did you ever try to defend yourself against one of your husband's unprovoked attacks?"

"Objection. Your Honor, we don't know whether or not the alleged attacks were provoked."

"Overruled."

"Cynthia," says Ms. Cohen, "did you ever do anything to provoke these vicious attacks? Did you ever attack your husband?"

"Never."

"Did you ever try to get help, try to persuade your husband to seek counseling?"

"Often, at first. But it only made him angrier. I soon re-

alized that to bring the subject up was to invite more violence."

"Did you ever consider getting a restraining order? Leaving him and getting a court order prohibiting him from con-
tacting you?"

"Yes, I did. I did consider that. In fact I contacted the
court and was offered a restraining order. And then I saw on
the news one evening how, in one month's time, three
women on Long Island, up in New York, three separate,
unrelated women who were being beaten and threatened by
their husbands got restraining orders. The reason it made
the news was that all three of them were dead. All three of
them were killed by the husbands or boyfriends they had
gotten the restraining orders against. After seeing that, I
knew it wasn't a realistic option. I knew Daniel might react
in the same way."

"Cynthia, how long did the beatings go on?"

"We were married in September of 'eighty-six. He began
beating me shortly after that. It went on, with increasing
frequency, until he died."

"Did he beat you the night he died?"

"He did. I thought he was going to kill me."

"Tell the jury what happened that night."

"We were camping. He became aroused. I resisted. He
beat me. He raped me. He beat me some more. I lost consciousness at one point, I don't know for how long. He
dragged me into our tent and told me that if I ever tried to
leave him he would kill me." I am not stuttering. I am
speaking clearly and calmly. I am making eye contact with
the jury. "I waited until I thought he was asleep. I didn't
know where I would go or how I would get there. I only
knew I had to get away from him. I was desperate. It took

forever, but finally I thought he was asleep. I was crawling out of the tent when he woke up and grabbed me. I don't know exactly what happened, how it happened. He began choking me, he had his hands around my neck and I couldn't breathe. Somehow I found his camping knife — it was there in the tent — and I got it in my hand and I stabbed him. I had to stop him. It was the only way. He was strangling me."

Ms. Cohen stands looking at me, at the jury, at me again. Letting it sink in. I can see myself from the jury box, as though I'm sitting there watching myself testify.

I think she is telling the truth.

My lawyer thanks me and passes the witness.

Mr. Marchander stands, walks to the front of the prosecution table. Leans on it.

"Good afternoon, Mrs. Mitchell."

"Good afternoon." This man is trying to get me locked up. He is trying to send me to prison.

"I apologize if some of my questions are difficult for you, Mrs. Mitchell, but we have to get to the substance of things here. Shall we proceed?"

"Please," I say.

"Daniel Mitchell, he was your first husband? You were married only once?"

"Yes."

"Prior to that, did you ever have any long-term relationships? Were you ever serious enough about anyone that you might have considered marriage?"

"I don't think I was, really. Perhaps once, but it didn't work out."

"Exactly how many lovers have you had over the years, Mrs. Mitchell?"

"Objection, Your Honor. Completely and totally irrelevant." She is righteously indignant, my lawyer.

"Sustained."

"Were you ever involved with a man who was violent toward you?"

"Other than my husband, no."

"You testified that he was abusive to you."

"I testified that he beat me, yes."

"Did you ever report any of this to the police?"

"No, I did not."

"Did you ever have to go to the hospital as a result of your husband's abusing you? Were your injuries ever sufficiently serious to warrant a trip to the emergency room?"

"There were times when I thought perhaps I should, Mr. Marchander, but I was too frightened, too ashamed."

"Did you ever need stitches?"

"I don't think so."

"Were any of your bones ever broken?"

"He broke my collarbone. He pushed me down the stairs once and I broke my collarbone."

"But you didn't go to the hospital?"

"No. I went to a physician's office. An orthopedic surgeon."

"What did you tell your friends when they saw you in a cast?"

"It didn't require a cast. I had a sling for a few days. I didn't see anyone during that time."

"But it was broken?"

"Yes. As the surgeon put it, if I had to break something, the collarbone was the way to go, because as long as both ends of the bone were still inside the body, it would heal by itself. The sling was only for comfort."

"Isn't it true, Mrs. Mitchell, that there were never any severe injuries, that your husband never physically injured you to the point that you had to seek hospitalization?"

"What I said, Mr. Marchander, is that I chose not to go to the hospital because I was afraid and ashamed."

"So you suffered in silence." He rolls his eyes.

"Yes, sir, I did. Looking back on it now, I realize it was foolish."

"Did you ever talk to anyone about what you say was happening in your marriage, Mrs. Mitchell? Your mother? Your sister? You never sought counseling?"

"I was afraid to talk to anyone. He cut me off from my friends and my family."

"In what way? Did you have a telephone in your home? Did he keep you locked up in a closet? Weren't you free to leave any time you wanted?"

"No, I was not. He told me if I ever tried to leave him he would kill me. And I believed him."

"Yes, but wasn't he talking about your leaving him permanently? Surely you were free to go to the store, to go to work, to visit friends."

"The only friends I had were Daniel's friends. When I first moved back and renewed some old acquaintances, he became enraged and did everything he could to keep me from socializing with anyone unless he was there and he had chosen the friends. He intercepted my phone calls, told people I was busy or working or just didn't feel like talking. Sooner or later they stopped calling."

"But none of these friends thought anything was wrong, did they? There was nothing about the relationship you had with Daniel, at least as far as these friends could see, that would cause them to suspect something was wrong. None of them investigated, none of them felt compelled to call the authorities."

"Your Honor," my lawyer interrupts, "the prosecutor is testifying, not cross-examining."

"Sustained." Judge Wulf has his bottom lip tucked in. He looks as if his thoughts are elsewhere.

"You never talked to your sister Alice about your relationship with your husband?"

"Not really, no."

"Mrs. Mitchell," he says, turning to face the jury, "your sister died shortly before you killed Daniel, did she not?"

"She committed suicide, yes."

"Took an overdose of pills?"

"Yes."

"Wasn't she having an affair with your husband? Weren't the two of them in love?"

"I don't think they were in love, no, sir."

"But they were having an affair? They were lovers?"

"I don't know if you can call it that, no. They were involved. I don't know to what extent."

"Mrs. Mitchell, do you know for how long they were, as you put it, involved?"

"No, sir, I don't. I don't think it was for more than a few months. From sometime around last Christmas until she killed herself."

He turns back to face me.

"You didn't kill her too, did you?"

I wait to see if my lawyer will object, but her gaze tells me to answer. Truth or Dare. I will never escape any of this.

"No, sir, I did not kill my sister."

"All right. All right. I can accept that. And I think the police have established that your sister's death was in fact a suicide. But isn't it true, Mrs. Mitchell, that you didn't kill your husband because he was beating you, but rather because you became murderously jealous when you found out about the affair? Isn't that why you killed him?"

I wonder how low this man will stoop. I sit looking at him and suddenly I see him on the floor, slithering up the aisle of the courtroom, his legs metamorphosed into a tail as he crawls on his belly like a reptile.

I do not answer.

"How did he come at you, Mrs. Mitchell? You've testified that your husband was strangling you. How did that happen exactly? Did you say something to enrage him? Was he drunk? What exactly happened?"

I look to my lawyer; she nods ever so slightly.

"I've told you how it happened. He decided we were going camping. We went deep into the woods, off the trail, not to a campsite. We were alone out there. He was all right, he was fine most of the evening. He seemed happy to be there."

"Go on."

"There was something, though, I can't say exactly, but just something that told me I had to move very carefully or he would go off on me. I'd seen it with him before. I knew the signs. And that's what happened. He wanted to make love. I was scared about being in the middle of nowhere with him. I thought he had brought me there to kill me. It turned out I was right."

"And how do you know that, Mrs. Mitchell? How did you know that he'd brought you there for that purpose? Maybe the guy just wanted to go camping. Maybe he found it romantic, being out in nature with his wife, and wanted to make love to you. Maybe he was thinking about the children that the two of you wanted so much. Could that have been the case? How did you know that he brought you there to kill you?"

I knew by the way he drove the car. I knew by the way he unloaded the camping gear, by the way he hammered the tent stakes into the ground. I knew by the way he ate dinner. It was in his voice. It was in his touch. Deliberate. Premeditated. Every move, premeditated. He had seen the whole night unfold a thousand times before. He had dreamed it. He had lived it in his mind.

"I didn't know for certain until he had his hands around my neck and was choking me to death. At that point, I felt reasonably sure he was trying to kill me."

My lawyer is trying not to cringe. I cannot help myself; I do not want to help myself. This man is trying to put me in prison. I defended myself, Mr. Prosecutor. I saved my life.

"Mrs. Mitchell," he says, suddenly angry, "did you not in fact stab your husband while he was asleep in the tent?"

"No, I did not."

"You admit that you killed him."

"In self-defense. I told you before, I don't know exactly how it happened. I only know that he was strangling me and somehow I got his knife and I stabbed him. It happened faster than I knew what was going on."

"How many times did you stab him?"

"I don't know. I don't actually remember stabbing him. I just don't remember."

"Seven times, Mrs. Mitchell. You stabbed your husband seven times."

"Objection."

"Overruled."

The prosecutor glares at me. Accuses me of murder for the jury.

"No further questions," he says.

I step down slowly, careful to look at the jury. I manage to get to the chair next to Ms. Cohen, next to Debra. She puts a hand on my arm.

"You did just fine," she says.

It is as though Daniel has just finished with me. I feel kicked, I feel hit, I feel cut and bruised. I am numb with pain. I look over at the jury. I hold my head up.

I close my eyes and listen to the voice of my lawyer, the voice of Judge Wulf. The voice of someone new. My lawyer has brought in an expert on violence, Dr. Trauner. His words echo in the courtroom, seem to come from across an ocean, floating over the sea of blue carpeting and into my tired ears. I breathe slowly and deliberately. *Be Here Now.*

"What is the cause?" my lawyer is saying.

"Myriad reasons," Dr. Trauner answers, his voice calm and confident. "The perpetrator is a loved one, the victim is ashamed of what's going on or fears retribution toward herself or another family member if she reports it to the police. The victim may well fear that the police won't care, won't do anything even if she does call. She may feel that she won't be believed because it's her word against her husband's or her lover's. There are rarely other witnesses, and even when there are suspicions, people are reluctant to get involved. Oftentimes friends feel helpless to do anything."

"Can you explain to us what happens to a woman who faces a violent episode?"

"What happens to anybody," he says. "When your life is threatened, your system goes into a fight-or-flight response: the heart rate increases, blood shunts to the extremities, your body prepares itself for defense or fleeing. But if someone is holding a gun to your head or otherwise immobilizing you, the response may be suppressed. You don't run. You don't fight. The arousal, though, still happens. It cannot be stopped or controlled. It's a survival mechanism. And it is very uncomfortable, so much so that each of us tries to avoid situations that will result in that response."

"So a woman whose life has been threatened will try not to be put in that situation again? How does that explain, or does it, why a woman such as my client might decide to stay with a husband who beats her and threatens her life?"

I want to scream.

"They stay because they are afraid of the consequences if they try to leave. They are sensitized to the cues that tell them violence is imminent. In fact, their threshold of sensitivity is changed because they have experienced violence. Even watching violent scenes on film becomes terrifying for them in a way it isn't for someone who has never experienced real-life violence. The battered woman does not want to face any more violence. She will do anything to avoid it. She will attempt to placate the batterer at any cost, and often the result is the development of post-traumatic stress disorder."

"Is that the same syndrome that plagues many Vietnam veterans? The result of having fought in a war?"

That is where I have been. I have been in a war.

"A conflict, yes. It is the result of combat. It's also very common among people who've been held hostage. There are several common factors. The hostages, like the soldiers and like battered women, are faced time and time again with life-threatening situations. There is no way to tell when the situations will arise, what might trigger them. One minute their captors are kind to them, the next, they're wondering if they are about to be executed."

"And what are the symptoms of PTSD?"

"As I mentioned before, increased arousal, a change of the arousal threshold — the response may occur with a much subtler cue than for a nonafflicted person. There are difficulties in concentrating. Extreme anxiety, nervousness. Sleep disturbances. The ability to reason, to think things through, is impaired. Problem-solving ability is impaired. The sufferer is prone to relive the event over and over and over whether it's disguised in the form of flashbacks, nightmares or the intrusion of violent fantasies during waking hours."

He comes at me as a dog.

"Where battered women are concerned, doctor, have you found a number of them tend to suffer from PTSD?"

"Oh, yes, indeed. A very high percentage of them have post-traumatic stress disorder."

"Why do they stay with their abusers?"

"Objection."

"Do you have an opinion, Dr. Trauner, with a reasonable degree of scientific certainty based on experience and practice, as to why battered women stay with their abusers? As to why Cynthia stayed with Daniel Mitchell long after she realized her life was in danger?"

"I do."

"And what is that opinion?"

"There are several factors, several reasons. Many stay because of the intermittent nature of the abuse. They love him. They believe he will change. Others because they feel, often correctly, that they have no place safe to go. They fear the batterer will hunt them down and harm them or their children. From the psychological perspective, we see what is called the predictable cycle of violence. Three stages. In stage one, tension reduction, the batterer subjects the victim to minor physical or verbal abuse. The woman responds by attempting to placate the batterer. Stage two is the acute battering incident — he beats her up. Stage three is characterized by loving contrition. The batterer is remorseful, he apologizes, often profusely, and vows never to harm the victim again. This stage may last for quite some time. And the intermittent nature of the violence leads to something we call traumatic bonding. The perception on the part of the battered woman, quite rightly, is that she is dominated by her batterer — he is in a position to bestow the favor of his kindness; she is less powerful, dependent on him for that favor. And the fact that there is no set pattern to the violence, that there is no particular way to tell what will trigger an attack, means that the victim will attempt to placate the batterer any time she believes that an attack is about to take place, whether that really is the case or not. If the attack doesn't take place, she thinks that her behavior somehow succeeded in preventing it. If the attack does take place, she wonders what she did wrong. This kind of 'partial reinforcement' of her behavior results in a strong emotional bond between victim and batterer — traumatic bonding. Many battered women cannot begin to think about leaving their batterer precisely because of this traumatic bond. It's known as the Stockholm syndrome — the very hand that takes you to your death is the hand that spares you. And when you think you are about to die and are spared, the resultant relief can lead to an actual fondness for that hand."

"And what happens if a woman pulls herself together and tries to leave? Are there any statistics?"

"The violence escalates when the victim attempts to leave. Batterers are extremely dependent on their victims. They need them. The prospect of living without them is terrifying. If they perceive a threat that their captive is escaping, they will increase the level of violence and they may also become suicidal."

I sit listening to Dr. Trauner explain why I stayed, why I cared, why I wanted to try again. Why I was afraid, why I was enthralled. Why I didn't just curl up and die. The jury looks and listens. How many times will this scene be repeated? How many juries are hearing this right now in courtrooms across the land?

"Recent estimates are about four million women a year," Dr. Trauner says.

"Assaulted?" asks my attorney.

"By the men they live with," he says, "husband or otherwise."

I did not even know.

Now it is Mr. Marchander's turn to pass without questions.

My lawyer calls the agent, the man she opted not to question earlier. Judge Wulf reminds him that he is under oath.

"You were the arresting agent, correct?" Ms. Cohen says.

"I was."

"Let me ask you, Agent Babcock, if you noticed anything unusual about my client at the time you arrested her."

"I did."

"And what was that, sir?"

"I noticed that she had numerous cuts and bruises on her face and neck."

"Did you offer medical assistance? Did you offer to take Cynthia to the hospital?"

"No, we did not."

"Why not?"

He shifts a bit in his seat, reaches to move the micro-phone away from his mouth.

"Well," he says, "frankly it looked like the damage had been done a few days earlier. And she seemed all right. We assumed they would see to it at the holding facility if there was a serious need for treatment. And she made no com-plaint."

"She didn't ask you to take her to the hospital?"

"No, ma'am, she did not."

"Agent Babcock, did you and your partner take any pho-tographs of Cynthia at the time you arrested her?"

"My partner did, yes."

"And were more photographs taken later?"

"I believe there were some taken at the holding facility, yes."

"Were these photographs retained as evidence in this case?"

"Yes, they were. That's procedure."

Ms. Cohen returns to the table and pulls from her satchel a stack of eight-by-ten photographs and a handful of Polar-oids. She shuffles through them quickly before turning to face Judge Wulf.

"Your Honor," she says, "may I approach the witness?"

Wulf nods. "Certainly."

She walks to the stand and shows the agent the photos.

"Agent Babcock," she says, "I'm showing you photo-graphs of Cynthia Mitchell and asking you if these are the Polaroid photographs taken by you and your partner at the time of her arrest and if these others are the photographs taken of her at the jail later that same day."

Agent Babcock examines them and tells her they are.

"Your Honor," Debra says, "I ask that these be marked as defense exhibits one through eight."

"Mr. Marchander?" says Judge Wulf.

"No objection," says Marchander. He does not even want to see them.

My lawyer takes the photos and walks to the jury box. She hands them, one by one, to the foreman.

"Look carefully," she says. The jurors pass them along, some cringing at what they see. I watch the man who resembles Daniel. He looks down at a photograph, looks up at me. He can't believe the damage he sees. He is still staring when my lawyer collects the photos and tosses them on the table in front of me, turns back to the jury.

She is saying something, but I do not hear her words. I look at the photos on the table. There I am in living color. There is the burn from Daniel's hands around my neck. There is the gash under my eye. There are the bruises that blossomed on my skin like flowers. I see shiitake mushrooms. I see chrysanthemums.

14

"By tonight," I say, "you'll once again have the luxury of a private room." I stand at my locker, my back to Kissy, and start to pull a few things together.

"Ahhh." She sighs. "But then who knows what kind of abomination will walk through that door and into my life?"

"You'll be fine." I don't know what else to say.

"Listen," she answers, "I'd say let's write, let's keep in touch, but the truth is, honey, I know you'll want to forget about this place and everyone in it as soon as you're out the door. I know I will if I ever get out."

"You'll get out."

"How'd you do it? How'd you get off?"

I raise the window and get a good firm grip on the wire mesh. I let myself feel it. Hard. Cold. Metal. I push my fingers through the diamonds of wire and try to rattle it. It holds firm, doesn't budge.

"I told them the truth," I say. "I told them it was self-defense."

"So did I," Kissy says. "And I've got *years* to do."

I want to say to her that perhaps if she hadn't enjoyed killing her lover she would not be doing time right now. But even as I think it, I realize it is self-righteous nonsense. Already I am trying to separate myself from the women who will remain in here, trying to convince myself that my case was special, that I should never have been arrested in the first place. Trying to assure myself that it was all just a mistake, though I know that Kissy and I did exactly the same thing. But we dealt with it differently. I understand now that she didn't come entirely clean. She lied about taking pleasure in the death of her lover.

"I'm sorry," I tell her. "I wish you were getting out with me."

I mean it. There is something resembling a smile on her face as her eyes fill with tears.

"Don't feel bad," she says. "The truth is I'm crying because it's you and not me."

"Is there anything you want? Consider whatever's in my locker yours," I say. "Is there anything I can send in for you?"

"Where are you going?"

"Only about twenty miles north of here," I say. "For a few weeks, anyway. Then, probably back to New York."

"Oh, God, Cyn. Are you sure?"

"I know. Noisy. Dirty. Full of maniacs."

"Just like Veritas."

"And you?"

"I guess I'll hang around here for a while and file appeals until they get tired and let me out. Maybe I'll look you up."

We both know this probably won't happen, but we pretend.

The merry-go-round is this: I take deep breaths while Dr. Hoffman listens to my heart. He taps my knees with a rubber hammer. He checks between my toes for signs of drug abuse. He looks in my ears and at my throat.

"You could use a little weight," he says, "but you're physically quite fit."

"Thanks, doctor," I say. "We'll just leave it at that, yes?"

He smiles at me — a real smile, genuine, not a baring of teeth.

Then he gives me a pass and I go, for the first time, out into the main compound, weaving my way through hundreds of prisoners moving toward lunch. I am amazed by the number of them. The hallway looks like Grand Central at morning rush hour, filled with reluctant commuters, walking fast to convince themselves they are headed toward something worthwhile.

I visit the dentist, whom I've never seen, and he signs my prerelease sheet. I visit the library, where I've never been, and the librarian signs that I have no overdue books. I return to Veritas, and Dr. Hoffman signs off as my case manager.

I am off the merry-go-round by one o'clock: my prerelease sheet has all the required signatures.

I go to my locker to finish packing and stand in front of it for I don't know how long until I realize there is not a single thing I want to take from this place. I notice a small envelope on the gray metal floor of the locker. I open it and there is my wedding band. There is a small piece of paper, too. A poem. "Lament for One White Girl."

I wad the paper into a tiny ball and walk down the hall to Coffee's room, where I push it through a diamond of wire. I tuck my wedding band into a pocket and go back to my room.

I am still waiting for someone to come and tell me I can leave when count time arrives. Time is moving both quickly and slowly. I cannot wait to leave. I am terrified of leaving.

Kissy and I stand next to each other in front of 310. We can hear Janna shuffling about in her locked room next door. At the door of the room on the other side of hers, Nina slouches against the frame. Her wrists are now covered with strips, see-through Band-Aids. She is less pale, but she has the look of someone who has just escaped from a serious automobile accident: her mind is still hurtling toward the moment of impact.

Across the hall, among others whose names I do not know but whose faces have by now become familiar, stand Herlinda, Emma, Lulu and Three Sheets.

It is mail call. The cute blond hack calls out names, and one by one the women get their letters. He hands Nina several letters and tries to give her a look, but she takes her mail without seeing him or the envelopes. Then, to my astonishment, "Mitchell."

I take the postcard he holds out. It says: "Greetings from Palisades Park, New Jersey."

I turn it over:

> The water's fine.
> xxxooo — Mother

I am relieved, and then something creeps in that feels suspiciously like elation. I've not felt it in such a long time that I'm unsure what it is. But she has made an escape. She has, as Herlinda would think of it, made a decision toward happiness.

Just before dinner, Svejk escorts me to Receiving and Discharge, in the basement of the main building. I hand over my paper. Svejk says, "You be good, now, girlie. No more sticking folks with knives." It occurs to me that Svejk is one of the fortunate few who has wound up precisely where he belongs: in the psychiatric ward of a federal prison.

I am sent upstairs, where I sit on a bench near the front door.

A taxi arrives and takes me down the long drive that leads to or from the prison.

The driver does not seem at all nervous.

15

The wind is up, blowing hard enough to force its way across the metal weather stripping at the bottom of the back door, making an eerie sound, as though someone is blowing randomly on a harmonica that plays only in a minor key.

I sit in the kitchen at a small marble-top café table that Daniel and I picked out together — I remember the day we shopped for it — but that now seems ill-made and unsuited for the room, like something dragged in at the last minute to accommodate unexpected and unwelcome company. The windsock next to the runway is taut, filled with air, and bends the slender pole to which it is attached. When the gusts kick up, the kitchen windows rattle.

The aroma of coffee is in the air, and I think of the woman named Coffee who is still in Veritas, of her and all the others who will be locked up for weeks or months or years and years and years. Coffee, I suspect, will probably go back to walking into stores and sticking guns in people's faces, taking their money. She has enough anger to last her lifetime. I think she will die violently, die young, though I hope she can avoid that fate.

The real estate agent arrives, on time to the minute. She is powdered and combed, plump and perfumed and nicely dressed. She takes out a little brass holder and places it on the kitchen counter and puts a stack of her business cards in it. She hands me one. I notice my wedding band next to the sink, where I always put it when I do the dishes. She sees me looking and says, "Maybe you should put that away. I can't be everywhere at once, and someone might take it. You'd be amazed what people are up to these days."

I wonder if she feels Daniel's presence as strongly as do I. It is different, though. I am in a house that he built, surrounded by his things, my things, our things. I take the wedding band and slip it in my pocket. I don't even remember wearing it last night. I don't remember doing the dishes. I don't remember eating. But I must have. The evidence is there.

I was scared at first, being in this place alone. But I know now that there is no menace.

For me at present, while I am alive on this earth, he exists only in memory. I choose whether or not to think of him. And how to think of him.

Today, I think of him with a large and terrible sadness, but I know it will not overwhelm me. It will never again overwhelm me.

I feel no guilt at having lied to the jury. I regret it, yes, but feel no guilt. It had to be that way. That part of it, too — my deception in court — was self-defense. I understood as soon as I was in custody, perhaps even before, that the Law has no room for those of us who strike back. I lied to the jury in self-defense.

I was defending myself against a man who so loathed himself that he was desperate for the love of another, and at the same time could not help trying to annihilate anyone who dared to love him.

I know that, had I not stopped him, he would have killed me. Eventually, he would have killed me. Or, as he did with Alice, driven me to kill myself.

And I know that had I told the truth about that night — that he was asleep — I would, like Kissy, be looking at years and years and years. In different circumstances? A different jurisdiction? I might be looking at a life sentence. I might be sitting on some state's death row.

"And if you'll follow me this way," I hear the agent say, getting closer, "we have a lovely kitchen and breakfast nook." Here they are. A couple, young and fresh-faced. The wife's belly round, holding life. Her eyes are alive with the future, his full of love for her and their child-to-be.

I smile at them and wonder, for an instant, if he hits her. But then I can see that he doesn't. There is no fear in her face. There is nothing false or painted-on about her happiness.

"How long have you lived here?" the husband asks. "Do you like the neighbors?"

"My husband was here for several years before I joined him," I say. I hope it doesn't sound rehearsed. "He got along wonderfully with everyone. We only got married a couple of years ago, but the neighborhood is wonderful. It's a great place for kids."

"You have children?" the wife asks.

"No." And then for some reason I add, "Not yet, anyway." I ask her when she is due.

"Four more months." She smiles.

"Good luck," I say, and she thanks me. They follow the agent out to the garage. She begins talking about airplanes and Rancho Milagro's private runway. I look out the kitchen window to the north end of it, where a sign says: COME TO A COMPLETE STOP AND CHECK FOR INCOMING AIR- CRAFT BEFORE CROSSING.

I am reminded of the third time Daniel took me flying. He borrowed a neighbor's Pitts Special, the red, white and blue biplane that I'd seen that first Christmas morning fly- ing upside down a few feet above the runway.

"No tricks," he said. "I'll tell you each maneuver, what I'm about to do."

The metal skin of the plane was so light that you could mash a dent into it by pressing with your fingers. The pas- senger seat was in front, right behind the propeller.

We were well up when I heard Daniel's voice through the earphones. He said, "Hold on to what you've got," and then the whole world turned upside down and I felt my stomach slide into the space where my lungs were supposed to be. I was lost, pinned to the seat by G-forces, helpless, whirling madly through the sky, and the runway flashed by overhead, merely inches below the windshield over the cockpit. It was only for an instant, but it seemed to go on forever. And then the sky straightened out and I could see the earth below us again. I felt as though my skin were breathing, expanding and contracting, filling with air and exhaling, and I heard Daniel's laughter, crackling like static in the headphones.

My knees weren't ready to take my weight when I climbed out of the Pitts; I wobbled around in circles, searching for a place where the earth wasn't undulating. Daniel stood there smiling at me, chortling, until I said, "You ever do that to me again and I'll barf all over the inside of your cute little plane."

"Aw, come on, Cynthia," he said, putting his arm around my shoulders. He walked me toward the house. "Anyway," he said, "it's not my plane."

I never flew with him after that. But I wouldn't have anyway. That was early in the marriage, just before the beatings began.

I see them outside the kitchen window now, walking the property, the wind forcing them to lean into it as they go. The husband puts his arm around the wife, helping her keep her balance. Mother always called it merciless, the wind in Texas.

I hope New Jersey isn't disappointing her. I hope she realizes that she still has a large part of her life to enjoy, even if things didn't get off to such a great start. She tried to tell me once what it had been like for her, but something held her back, and I didn't even know what questions to ask, much less how to phrase them.

I know it took an effort for her to visit me in Veritas. It is not the kind of place she would ever want to be seen going into or coming out of. But there she was, even if it was only for a few minutes.

Now it will not be necessary for her to tell me. Now I have learned for myself. It was the same sort of thing, I know. The same crushing betrayal.

I know from looking at her photo album. He said marry me and I'll love you forever. Marry me and we'll have the most wonderful family on earth. Marry me and I'll treat you like a queen. Marry me and our happiness will know no bounds. He knew how to touch her to make her feel wanted.

She loved him. She married him. And when the honeymoon was over, she found herself living a nightmare in the shadow of his brutal, murderous rage. How dare she love him. How dare she.

The front door opens and closes. The agent comes in.

"They've made an offer," she says excitedly. "It's not what we're asking, but I think it's one you should consider. It's a reasonable offer."

"Then let's take it," I say.

"Don't you want to know what it is?"

"Oh, of course," I say.

She says a number. She says we could make a counteroffer. I tell her that's not necessary.

She brings them in, all smiling, all smiles. We shake hands and off they go to the bank. Off they go into the future.

The agent is so excited that she leaves her cards on the kitchen counter.

There's a stack of mail on the dining room table. I wonder if it was transported in one of my mailbags. Special offers, sale notices. A bill from my lawyer. *I, too, may already be a winner.*

It all stays unopened, stacked there on the table like someone's forgotten dishes.

I wander to the bedroom, to Daniel's closet, which smells of dry-cleaning fluid. His pilot uniforms hang in a row, immaculately pressed.

Too much has happened too fast. I know I have not yet realized it all. It has been almost four months since I killed my husband. It hasn't even been four months since I killed my husband. It doesn't seem to matter how I say it; it still jars me. Perhaps someday I will be able to say it without feeling the electric jolt that forces me to mentally shake myself. Perhaps someday I will not have to say it at all.

I remember the night with Dr. Hoffman when he said I was grieving over the loss of my victimization. I wonder if he will ever be able to say that to Kissy. I wonder if Nina is even at this moment shuffling around the dayroom in her bathrobe, looking for someone to light her cigarette. I wonder if Emma is still afloat.

I have mourned the loss of my victimization. No one can force me to do anything anymore. I am responsible for my own decisions. My own choices.

But I have not yet figured out how to grieve for Daniel. I do not know if I will be able to. I don't even know if I need to, because I understand now that I grieved for the loss of his promise a long, long time ago. I grieved for the loss of the man I thought he was, the man he presented himself as, the man he wanted to be. The first time he hit me was the end of any chance we might have had. I could not admit it then, but that was the end.

Tomorrow I will call Goodwill, call the movers, call an old friend up north. By the end of the week I will be on the road to New York. I will not get on a plane and be hurtled toward the city in a metal tube that rips through the sky like a bullet. I will take my time, drive slowly, stop to enjoy lunch in small-town restaurants. Maybe I'll even swing through New Jersey.

ABOUT THE AUTHOR

Kim Wozencraft is the author of the best-selling novel *Rush*, now a major motion picture starring Jennifer Jason Leigh. She holds a master of fine arts degree from Columbia University and her work has appeared in *The Best American Essays*. She lives in New York with her husband, the writer Richard Stratton, and their son, Maxwell.